BRIDPORT PRIZE ANTI

EXTRACTS FROM THE NOVI

JUDGE
Victoria Hislop

First published in 2021 by Redcliffe Press Ltd
81g Pembroke Road, Bristol BS8 3EA

e: info@redcliffepress.co.uk
www.redcliffepress.co.uk
Follow us on Twitter @RedcliffePress

Follow The Bridport Prize:
Follow us on Twitter and Instagram @BridportPrize
www.bridportprize.org.uk
www.facebook.com/bridportprize

ISBN 978-1-911408-85-7

British Library Cataloguing-in-Publication Data
A catalogue record for this book is available from the British Library

Typeset in 10.5pt Times

Typeset by Addison Print Ltd, Northampton
Printed by Hobbs the Printers Ltd, Totton

Contents

Good news in bad times

In these pandemic times good news has been in short supply, yet the fact we have been reading more than ever is surely something to smile about. Settling down with a good book proved a welcome escape from the dystopian world that became reality. Sales of fiction and ebooks flourished as we rediscovered the simple pleasure of wanting to know more about the people, places and lives unfolding in the pages before us.

Despite everything, this year brought many talented writers with fresh voices telling stories that enthralled our judges and made the final cut painfully difficult.

We know that being able to read new writers who trust us with their words is a genuine gift. Thank you to all the writers. For those not featured here, please keep telling your stories. Ask anyone in publishing and they will say a novel is a marathon not a sprint. And writers are always in training.

We hope these highly original winning extracts live long in your memory as they will in ours.

You are in for a treat.

Where are they now?

Polly Crosby was our novel runner up in 2018 with *The Illustrated Child*. The novel was published last year in the UK and US. Her next novel, *The Unravelling* is out in 2022. Polly has cystic fibrosis: 'I know how hard it can be. I was lucky enough to be given opportunities, and I want to pay this forward.' She has created bursaries for writers who are disabled or living with a long term illness.

Deepa Anappara won our novel award in 2017 and *Djinn Patrol on the Purple Line* was published in 2020 in the UK and US. It was long listed for the Women's Prize for Fiction and shortlisted for the JCB Prize for Literature. It was a New York Times Editors' Choice, a Val McDermid New Blood pick, and a BBC Radio 2 Book Club pick. Deepa was selected as one of The Guardian / Observer ten best debut novelists of 2020.

Eve Smith was shortlisted for our novel award in 2017 and her debut novel *The Waiting Rooms* was published last year. Waterstones hailed Smith 'an exciting new voice in crime fiction' and the novel was The Guardian's book of the month.

Carolyn Kirby, shortlisted for her novel in 2016 saw her most recent book *When We Fall* chosen by the Times and Sunday Times as one of the best historical novels of 2020.

Kelleigh Greenberg-Jephcott was our 2015 novel award winner with *Swan Song*. The book was published in 2018 to many accolades: it was longlisted for the women's prize for fiction, won The Society of Authors McKitterick prize and was shortlisted for the Goldsboro Books Glass Bell Award. The Times wrote, 'this novel never flags, and never forgets the duty to entertain.' The Guardian described it as 'a skilled and sparkling debut.'

Coming soon

Ryan O'Connor's *The Voids*; Nicholas Ruddock's *Last Hummingbird West of Chile;* Sean Lusk's *The Second Sight of Zachary Cloudesley.*

Find out more at www.bridportprize.org.uk

Novel Award Partners

The Bridport Prize is proud to work in partnership with the following organisations in the delivery of the Peggy Chapman-Andrews Award for a First Novel.

A.M. Heath Literary Agents

Founded in 1919 by Audrey Heath and Alice May Spinks, two women who challenged the conventions of publishing, we are a London literary agency still very much driven by a passion to help writers who want to shift, shape or enrich the wider cultural conversation, and provide irresistible entertainment.

Championing our clients' writing remains at the heart of what we do. As well as a century of experience, we bring energy, ambition, and a keen eye for detail to our work.

We're always looking out for original ideas combined with great quality writing, and we work with the Bridport Prize to encourage emerging writers. By helping to draw up the long list and shortlist for the Peggy Chapman-Andrews Award for a First Novel, we aim to support the best new novelists to find publishers and readers across the world.

Website: www.amheath.com
Twitter: @EuanThorneycrof / @AMHeathLtd

Tinder Press

Tinder Press is an imprint of Headline, which in turn is a division of Hachette – one of the largest publishing groups in the UK. Tinder Press was launched in 2013, and is Headline's home for literary fiction, a space where classy, intelligent writing can thrive. Our stable of prize-winning and bestselling authors includes Maggie O'Farrell, Andrea Levy, Patrick Gale, Deborah Moggach, Chloe Benjamin and Guy Gunaratne. Our authors have won or been listed for prizes including the Costa, Women's Prize, Dylan Thomas, Man Booker, Goldsmiths, Jhalak, Caine Prize, Orwell and Wellcome.

Tinder Press prides itself on its bespoke approach to publishing, which starts with an editor's passion, which then galvanises the whole publishing house. Our authors are always at the heart of everything we do, and our aim is to nurture their writing and build careers that will endure.

Website: www.tinderpress.co.uk
Twitter: Tinder Press / @maryanneharring

The Literary Consultancy

The Literary Consultancy is the UK's first and leading writing consultancy, offering editorial advice and manuscript assessment since 1996. Its aim is to provide honest, professional editorial feedback to writers to give them a better sense of whether and where their work might fit into the ever-changing market.

TLC and its team of world-class professional readers work with writers writing in English at all levels, across all genres. A popular 12-month mentoring programme, Chapter and Verse, supports writers to completion of a book project, alongside a suite of creative and practical events, and a yearly writing retreat, Literary Adventures.

The Literary Consultancy believes that fair, objective feedback can unlock the creative potential of writers at all levels, from emerging to professional. To achieve this, it focuses on cultivating the personal value of writing, equipping writers with the context, confidence, and skills they need to thrive and flourish.

Email: info@literaryconsultancy.co.uk
Website: literaryconsultancy.co.uk
Twitter: @TLCUK
Facebook: The Literary Consultancy

VICTORIA HISLOP

Judge's Report

The winner of the Peggy Chapman-Andrews First Novel Award is *The House of Broken Bricks* by Fiona Williams.

The writer describes with convincing intimacy a mixed-race marriage and lays bare the complexities of the relationship which arise through both circumstances and skin colour. The couple's problems are painfully intensified by the death of one of their twins and a move to deepest rural England.

The themes of loss and deracination are powerfully evoked through the use of metaphor and through the experiences of day to day life, particularly for Jess, the wife and mother of the two boys. Despite the themes with which she deals, Williams is never sentimental. And she delivers surprise after surprise, not least the opening, which is in the voice of the little boy, Sonny (who has already died). It's a shocking but powerful first page and from that moment it only gets better.

The writing itself is at times utterly magical and lyrical – but never self-indulgent. There is a restraint that I really admired. The descriptions are often very sensory and poetic and there is a sense that the writer really knows the landscapes and the locations in which the characters find themselves.

The book mixes beauty and pain in a truly remarkable way and after the opening 30,000 words, I was left with a strong desire to know what happens in the end. For me this is the best kind of story telling – characters I genuinely care about, and a narrative that demands to be followed. Congratulations, Fiona Williams

The runner up for the prize is *Portrait of a Family* by Tamara Henriques.

From the opening sentence: "The day my sister and I burnt the house down, our mother, Margot was out with her dealer, Cosmo." I was totally hooked!

In this story we have another set of twins, this time girls. And we see much of the story through their eyes – which is superbly managed. They have sweet, funny, engaging and totally convincing child-voices – that are nicely written without being remotely over-cute. I believed totally in the characters of the children, but of course most importantly in the harassed and mildly irresponsible artist-mother. She is a wonderfully flawed human being, but all the more likeable for that and I hugely enjoyed reading about her situation. The fraught relationship with her husband lurks like a shadow in the early chapters, very subtly alluded to, but making us want to know and understand more.

There are some glorious metaphors – I particularly loved "The key is still there, heavy and ornate, like a piece of antique cutlery." But Henriques never over-writes. There is humour (which is hard to do well) and the story is always engaging and never dull. This is a novel where I found myself turning pages quickly to find out what happened next.

Highly Commended are:
The Arctic Vault – Helga B. Viegas
I found this a sweeping, ambitious and very timely dystopian novel. There are some brilliantly written descriptions of a new and very terrifying world where everyone is micro-chipped and food is created not grown. It is a frighteningly believable vision of the future and I was gripped from the very beginning.

Me, Rosa and Bridget Bird – Gemma Seltzer
A story of the complexities of female friendships. The writer explores relationships between sisters as well as friends, in particular a love triangle that endures over many years and captures with great acuity the jealousies and insecurities that exist in the female mind.

The Girl in the Glass House – Mónica Parle
This is a richly evocative and very original story set on the US-Mexico border. The descriptions of place and period are ambitious, but generally successful. I was transported to another time and place.

Walk in my Shadow

Synopsis

*Raya has lived her life in the shadow of her father's disappointment and fear of her husband **Sohrab**, only finding solace in work and her poetry. She finally has the courage and decides to leave him when Sohrab refuses to accept their gay son. But a racist attack leaves him fighting for his life before she tell can him. **Zafar**, author and art gallery owner unexpectedly meets Raya at the hospital. The only woman Zafar has loved.*

Two years earlier, Raya and Zafar meet at a party in London. They discover the paths of all three have crossed at a wedding in Dhaka three decades ago. After which, Sohrab asks Raya to marry him following a brief courtship. His Pakistani roots reopen old wounds as Raya's uncle was killed by the Pakistani army during Bangladesh's war of independence. Raya's father refuses to give his consent, only agreeing when her grandmother intervenes. Their relationship changes irrevocably.

Over time, Raya finds Sohrab ambitious and uncompromising and discovers his affair with his first wife. When she threatens to divorce him he frightens her into believing he will get sole custody of the children. Raya stays for their sake.

After the anniversary party, Zafar pursues Raya. Their relationship evolves from friends to lovers and she wants to be with him. But Zafar rejects her. He realises his mistake and is unable to make amends due to his father's sudden death after which it is too late.

At the hospital they agree to meet the following day. She does not come as Sohrab dies but Zafar leaves thinking she has not forgiven him.

Meanwhile Raya emerges stronger and publishes her book of poetry.

They meet again after Zafar learns of Sohrab's death. He asks Raya to sign her book of poetry. No words are necessary.

PART ONE
Chapter 1

They didn't make love anymore. It stopped years ago and somehow became sex, that is when they had the time or inclination. At first, it was hard to acknowledge and even harder to accept that they were sleeping together to fulfil a physiological need. Nothing more. Years of intimacy give you a sense of how each other's body works and reacts – like old instruments, they were fine-tuned to one another. And gradually even that stopped. These days they didn't have sex anymore either.

The warmth of Sohrab's body next to hers was familiar and comforting. Over the years he was a habit that Raya had been unable to break.

The sound of the city waking from its slumber seeped in through the windows. The golden fingers of the sun reaching inside the crack between the curtains caressing the room with its light.

She propped herself on her elbow and looked down at his sleeping face, his mouth slack, right arm raised above his head. He was still a handsome man even after all these years, a hint of a stubble accentuating his strong jawline, soft hair falling carelessly over his forehead. The grey was gradually usurping the black. He stirred then turned over and fell back asleep.

She was standing on the edge of a precipice, all she needed to do was jump. Raya pulled the covers off and as noiselessly as she could, made her way to the bathroom for her shower before Sohrab awoke.

Chapter 2

Zafar touched his card on the machine, waited for the green lights to flash then placed it back inside his leather wallet. It was a good thing he had checked in the fridge and discovered there was no milk, eggs, or even bread and ordered a Chinese delivery from his favourite restaurant then legged it to the shop before it closed. Tom was a perfect houseguest except for his black hole of an appetite which meant Zafar frequently came home to a much-depleted cupboard. He had forgotten the last time there were any leftovers. But with almost twenty-five years of friendship behind them, it wasn't something he begrudged his mate.

Suleiman, the cheery Lebanese owner of the shop offered him a plastic bag which he declined, placing all his items of shopping in his backpack. It was one less plastic bag in the world. He waved his thanks and headed for the door. The only other occupant in the shop was a man in a tweed jacket who was inspecting two brands of jam with great concentration. You would think he was buying a house, not a fruit condiment. Zafar resisted the urge to take one of the glass jars out of the man's hand and put it on the counter ending his obvious dilemma. Instead, he said, 'I'd go for the raspberry,' to the man, who looked even more bewildered. Satisfied, Zafar stepped into the darkness of the night, his breath catching in his throat from the cold. The air was bracing, a whisper of a breeze rustling the leaves on the treelined street and he zipped his jacket up to his chin.

Staying in on a weekend alone. Eating a takeaway alone. Going to bed alone. How the mighty are fallen. But it was a form of self-inflicted penance. One he was willing to do.

Chapter 3

It was surprising that there was no one around. Raya put it down to it being a Wednesday evening with people wallowing in mid-week blues, counting the hours till the weekend began. The only person they passed was a man walking his dog, an excitable little thing with its tail wagging, tongue out. And one which they couldn't resist stopping to stroke. When Sohrab asked what breed the curly-haired ball of excitement was, the answer was 'Cockapoo', a crossbreed between a Cocker Spaniel and Poodle. Poor little fellow.

'At least it's not a Peekapoo, you know a Pekingese and a Poodle or a Yorkipoo... hang on what do you think a Husky and a Corgi would be? Horgi? Chusky?' she said tilting her head to one side. This elicited a smile and a shake of the head from Sohrab.

The stillness of the night was calming – unlike the turmoil taking place inside her head. Raya tried to compose her thoughts. There were so many things she wanted to say – needed to say. Sohrab Hussain was a man who required logic and rationale. Arguments fuelled by emotion would make him disengage and look at her in the way he often did, like that gauche seventeen-year-old he had met in Dhaka all those years ago. She had rehearsed the entire conversation over and over in her head, her decision, his reaction, her response. A waltz with words instead of music. Neither of them spoke as they walked side by side.

The only sound around them was the crunching of gold and russet leaves underfoot as they strolled across the grass and onto the footpath towards the top of the hill – an ideal place for photographers to capture the London skyline. A selfie-taker's paradise or for lovers to watch the sunset, sitting side by side, holding hands.

Dinner had been pleasant enough though Raya found herself distracted for most of it.

Their hosts were delighted that Sohrab had agreed to go in the first place, and he hadn't disappointed. On the contrary, he was on good form and she watched him captivate his audience with an ease borne from the knowledge of his own intellect and charm. A glimmer of the man she used to know. This manifestation showed itself in bursts though usually reserved for others. They both played their parts well – at least in public. Actors par excellence.

'I never get tired of this view,' she said, her sigh audible in her silent surroundings.

There was always the same sense of awe when she reached the crest of the hill where London lay sprawled before her. Brushstrokes of grey broke up the deeper blue expanse of night sky. Apparently not a time when stargazing or rather skyline gazing featured heavily on people's minds. They might as well have been the only two people left on the planet.

'Lovely,' said Sohrab perfunctorily as he checked his phone.

The night sky was devoid of stars but illuminated by city lights spread across the horizon. White lights interspersed with red and the occasional blue ones blinking in the distance. The cover of darkness had a way of hiding a city's flaws, cloaking it in a semblance of respectability. She wondered what secrets were hidden behind the shining lights in the distance. If eyes were the windows of the soul then maybe if she looked behind the bright lights, she would find that windows were the eyes into people's lives.

They reminded her of the Christmas decorations and fairy lights Irfaan and Samar used to put up when they were kids. Kids – they had stopped being that a while ago. It was as if Raya had woken up one day to find her children had been replaced by two adults who resembled them.

The London Eye loomed in the distance. Irfaan had thought it was a giant Ferris wheel when they had taken him and Samar for the first time. The disappointment of realising the pace of the cantilevered wheel was what he claimed 'slower than a snail going backwards' had been assuaged by a trip to the London Aquarium and an ice cream.

'Are you done? Can we go now?' Sohrab's deep voice broke into her thoughts. He shoved his hands into his coat pocket warding off the cold.

'Yes, fine. Let's go.' At least he had put his phone away. It was an extra appendage he had acquired over the years.

Sohrab started walking and Raya took in the view one more time before following him down. Maybe they should have taken a cab and gone home as he suggested but she knew she wouldn't get the time or privacy in a taxi, especially with a driver listening in. The journey wasn't long enough for the conversation she needed to have and once they got home he would disappear into his study or go to bed. Moreover, she didn't want him to have the option of slamming the door with an 'end of discussion' and walking out. She had put it off for long enough.

'Well, I hope you're wearing shoes you can walk in? I doubt you'll be able to do it in high heels,' he said glancing at her feet when she brought up the idea of walking through the park after dinner. Under other circumstances, Sohrab noticing what shoes she was wearing would have made her wonder if he had been body-snatched. If she had asked him to close his eyes and describe her attire, Raya suspected he would have failed. Her

14

response was to point to her not very elegant but comfortable black boots. She had come prepared. So here they were in the park. Right now, Sohrab was her captive audience.

Her phone vibrated in her pocket. She checked the message knowing what it would say, 'Have you told him yet?' but slipped it back in without replying. It was pointless before broaching the topic with Sohrab.

She was tired. Tired of being defined by others. Daughter, sister, wife, mother, friend, confidante, lover – multiple hat wearer extraordinaire. It was easy to lose herself in the sea of different identities.

'Look I wan—'

'Raya don't forget the car's being picked up tomorrow for its MOT. I have to leave early for a meeting.'

MOTs was not the conversation she wanted to have. It was typical that he had assumed she would be the one staying at home for the pick-up. Part of her wanted to tell Sohrab that he could wait as she had a meeting in the morning – which she didn't.

'Don't worry, I'll stay till they take the car. I need it back by Friday though. Taking Amma to the GP,' she found herself replying.

'They said they'd drop it off the same day.'

'Yeah, assuming they don't find any major faults with it. Last time it was the tyres, before that it was the brakes or something. Uff! You should have checked with me before booking.'

'Orey baba! Sorry for trying to help,' he said placing his palms together.

There was no point arguing. Some people had the knack of making you feel they were doing you a favour even when the gesture or act in question was one that was neither requested nor required. Raya kept walking.

'What's up with Amma? She didn't mention anything to me.'

'She wants to see if the GP can refer her to a specialist for her eyes. They seem to be getting worse. She's pretty impressive for her age you know.'

He glanced sideways at her, 'You trying to show me up? You look after Amma better than I do.'

Not that it was hard. If anything she had always been a pillar of strength and wisdom. Since they got married, he had slowly abdicated responsibility for his mother. Initially, he said it was because Raya knew how to deal with her. It wasn't as if she needed dealing with or looking after. Widowed at an early age, Amma had brought up her two children as a single parent in the UK, unthinkable for a Bangladeshi woman, especially in the seventies. Instead of packing her bags and going back, she had worked as a teacher till she retired then set up a small catering company only stopping a few years ago because of her declining health. Independent and unapologetic – qualities Raya admired in Amma. In a way, she got on better with her than her own mother, whose life still revolved around socialising and swanning from one party to another, Raya's idea of torture. Age had not managed to dull her mother's joie de vivre or rather jouissance de parties.

In the early stages of their marriage, her mother-in-law had insisted that Raya learn to drive telling her it was a life skill. Everyone needed to be able to cook, drive a car, and do their taxes. Advice Raya had passed down to her children.

These days, Amma's eyesight wasn't what it used to be and she was less confident getting about by herself. They had tried to coerce her into living with them but being self-sufficient all her life, it was something she hadn't yet agreed to.

'Don't allow yourself to become so dependent on a man, or in fact anyone, that they become indispensable. Because they're not.' This advice had been imparted years ago and it had always stuck in Raya's head but recently more so.

'I've been meaning…I really want to talk to you about something…' The neatly prepared, rehearsed mental dialogue was unravelling. MOTs and trips to GPs hadn't been part of it. Then again, life was never neat. It was messy and unpredictable. Her palms were uncharacteristically sweaty and she wiped them on her coat.

'I'm listening,' he said but she could see his gaze was elsewhere. It was annoying that even now he couldn't give her a minute of his undivided attention. She followed his eyes and saw a group of boys or youngish men walking up the hill towards them. They were pushing and shoving each other. Their voices carried in the silence, raucous laughter ringing out.

Sohrab turned and took her hand. 'Let's go, just keep walking.' Even without this unusual display of protectiveness, Raya absorbed his uneasiness and she looked around to see if there were any other people nearby but there was no one.

Soon they were close enough to spot bottles in their hands. One of them was spraying the others with what Raya guessed was beer. A knot formed itself in the pit of her stomach.

Part of her wanted to ignore them and keep walking. The 'If I don't look at them, they won't see me' thought process was immediately replaced by the 'show no fear' one. The programme she had watched about bears on some nature channel popped into her head. There had been a segment on what to do if you encountered one. She tried to remember if you were supposed to look them in the eye and stand your ground. Or was it the other way round and you had to avoid eye contact? She ended up smiling at the young men in an attempt to hide her growing sense of panic. They were probably messing about.

'Oi look, it's Mr and Mrs Paki!' said a boy wearing a black puffer jacket, his floppy blonde hair partially covering his eyes. He stopped in front of them. The three others came and blocked their way. Sohrab tried to guide her away but they moved to create a semicircle around them.

ANDREW BONNER

The Long Field

Synopsis

The Long Field *is a literary-commercial crossover about a man returning to Donegal one month after missing his father's funeral, and more than thirty years since leaving his homeland.*

Having departed Ireland in the early 1960's vowing never to go back, John-Joseph is forced to return in the late 1990's when his father, Mick, dies suddenly, leaving no will. In the process of returning to a country that has become strange to him, John-Joseph embarks on a psychological odyssey through the landscape of his childhood, where every encounter revives memories he thought were long dead.

As he journeys around his old haunts, John-Joseph remembers the devastation caused by his mother's death to meningitis when he was a baby, and his father's stricken response. He learns to forgive Mick, whose silent melancholy he mistook for weakness, when he learns that his father's refusal to leave their farm was the only way he knew to fulfill a promise made to his dying wife. John-Joseph discovers too that his urge to leave this place was nothing more than a childish attempt to run away from a perceived danger but, by so doing, he ran from the only person who might understand his fear and pain. Whether or not he comes back to the Long Field to retain his father's pride and joy, will determine if he can also accommodate a past that includes the loss of his mother.

In this story a man learns that escaping the sadness of his youth is no guarantee of a happy life, and that people can choose to define themselves by their sense of a place or by their absence from it. This is a novel about how we can change the meaning of our lives by reclaiming the spaces from which we have chosen to be exiled.

1

The solicitor had been talking about the three animals for at least five minutes and how important it was to be rid of them, but now turned to the matter at hand.

Your father left no will, John-Joseph, but being his only son, you are entitled to the estate, comprising of the home-place, which is a small cottage and some byres, and thirty-or-so acres of land. And the three animals, of course.

Stacks of manila foolscap files were crammed on to the shelves behind the solicitor who, pausing to make sure that he was following, leaned forward in the high-backed, fake-leather executive chair which made demur, fart-like squeeks every time it moved. The solicitor's hands clasped together on the desk, and he saw that the solicitor wore silver cufflinks in the shape of Celtic crosses. Very neat.

Does that sound about right to you?

Yes, that sounds about right, he said.

Now, there appears to be very little cash in your father's bank account, but his Credit Union monies should cover the funeral expenses. You might need to speak to Kilpatrick, the undertaker, about those burial costs, but I do have some back up paperwork for the wake and various items. The solicitor handed him an A4 envelope. In here, the solicitor said.

He looked inside and saw that it was filled with printouts, bills and till receipts.

It's not a huge amount, said the solicitor, just some expenses from the wake and a bit of animal feed. You know, I wouldn't be surprised to find a plastic bag full of cash in an airing cupboard or a shed somewhere, as is the way with men of his generation. God knows, I heard a tale about a daughter who was visiting the hospital, after her father had some minor operation for whatever it was, and when the old boy took a stroke and died suddenly in the bed, she didn't tell any of her brothers or sisters. Not a one. She drove up to the father's house to get the shoe box under his bed with a hundred thousand in it, and took the lot. Life-savings, John-Joseph: every last punt saved in a shoe box. Hard to believe. Of course, there was no official record the money ever existed, nor that she had taken it but everyone in the county knew. She bought herself a lovely Toyota Corolla.

The solicitor paused and said, maybe you should take a look around the place for something like that.

He wasn't quite sure what to do with this information, so nodded along.

I suppose I should, he said.

Good, so. I shall get started on the probate and, in the fullness of time, the farm and the dwelling-house will be yours. Now, the things is, due to your father's intestacy, the granting of probate could take several weeks, if not months, but you should contact an estate agent now: I will need a valuation in order for that whole process to be completed. These things always take longer than you think, so it's best to get started on that as soon as you can. I believe it's Morris who looks after estate valuations over there, and I shouldn't be surprised if you got rather a good estimate. Land prices are very much heading in the right direction just now; developers looking for plots all the time and farmers are just taking the money and enjoying themselves with it, quite frankly.

Ok.

When the valuation comes in, we would then need to talk about inheritance tax issues, for which I can recommend a very good accountancy practice here in the town. They would talk you through it, and obviously the estate agents can advise on the various levels and brackets that come into play.

Ok, I'll just wait and see, he said.

Now, much as it will be an irrelevance to your overall valuation, you should sell those three animals. Just to have them out of the way and tidied up on the accounts side of things. They're not worth a great deal, it would be fair to say, and by the time you've paid out for the vets and feed and bedding, and all the rest of it, you would be spending money with absolutely no hope of a return. Your father's neighbour, Fergus McCauley, is looking after them, I believe.

I'm not sure, but I'll take your word for it, he said. It's not that hard of a job though, is it?

Fair question, said the solicitor, but you might not appreciate the work involved, if you don't mind me saying. Not being so experienced in animal management yourself.

The solicitor halted his flow.

It's a Department of Agriculture thing, you know, nothing personal. And Fergus would need to be relieved of his duties quite soon as I'm sure this must be rather burdensome for him.

Fergus owned the farm next door to his father's and, being an old friend conveniently located, had volunteered to look after the animals in those days after Mick had died when the neighbours were trying to track him down and he was busy missing the wake and the funeral.

They are now the estate's responsibility, which is to say, of course, your responsibility, and if they were to wander on to a neighbour's land or, God forbid, they injured some, you know, day-trippers, you would be held liable.

He couldn't imagine that a single 'day-tripper' had been up there in the Entire History of Ireland, but maybe things had changed since he'd been away.

Yes, I understand, he said. What would happen if I just kept them?

The solicitor paused.

Are you planning to take them back to England with you? Or maybe you are thinking of staying for a while?

He thought for a few seconds but couldn't find a suitable answer.

Well, he said, I can't stay very long. I understand there's a lot to sort out, but I only have a week off work.

I see, said the solicitor. And what is it you do for a living, out of interest?

I'm a manager in a paper plant. We get magazines or books nobody can sell and pulp and turn them into cardboard boxes or toilet paper, or whatever.

He always said he was a Manager because people didn't warm so quickly to a Factory Foreman.

Having no personal connection with, or anecdotes relating to, the paper-pulping business, the solicitor drew a total blank at this biographical detail, so decided to move the conversation on.

Well, ok, whatever you decide is fine by me, the solicitor said. In the mean time, whether you keep the animals or not, I should also advise you to get some farm insurance, making sure it includes Public Liability Insurance.

The solicitor said the last three words very slowly, with the capital letters all in, as if he were speaking to an infant foreigner.

Please do make that a priority. You wouldn't believe the commotion that comes with a twisted ankle on private land these days.

Those day trippers, he said.

Well, it could be anyone, in fairness, said the solicitor, missing his little joke entirely.

Ok, can I ask a question, he said.

Of course, fire away.

What if nobody had found me? You know, to tell me he was dead. What would have happened?

The solicitor seemed torn between striking an avuncular tone or sticking with the professional approach. The chair squeeked out a couple of tiny farts as the solicitor shuffled in his seat.

Well, John-Joseph, let me say this: attempts to find you would have continued apace and, this being a small community with very long arms, you would have been found. Of that, I have no doubt. And, you know, it wasn't really so difficult in the end up. But to answer your question: your father's property would have simply defaulted to the State, there being no other natural heirs that we know of.

He nodded again.

The solicitor watched him for a moment and said, John-Joseph, please be assured that the farm doesn't actually have to be yours. It's not a life-sentence you're looking at. Are you sure you want me to proceed with the probate application for you?

He thought, well, why else would I be sitting here so he said, yes, of course, please, go on.

Ok, said the solicitor, then I suppose this is what you came for.

The solicitor slid a smaller white envelope towards him that had been sitting on the desk since he had arrived, and said, I believe this is the key to the front door of your father's house. Fergus's daughter left it over when she heard you were coming.

The envelope had *'Cullydawson Dwelling House'* written by hand on the front. He opened it and a single Yale key, attached to a souvenir key-ring from 'Sunny Bundoran', fell on to his palm.

Twenty-one again, he said.

Now, said the solicitor, I think that is about it – no, wait, what on earth is wrong with me today? I'll need your birth certificate and a copy of your father's death certificate. The Court of Probate need proof that you are the natural heir, that your father is indeed deceased and that you therefore have the right to dispose of his estate.

There's a hell of a lot to do, isn't there, he said.

And he tried to remember when he had last seen his own birth certificate. He must have had one at some point, if only to get a passport, but that was a long time ago and he hadn't renewed it in ages. Being on the boats and then settling in England, he didn't carry stuff like that around with him. He wondered how he would find such a thing now but didn't want to appear ignorant, so said nothing.

Alert to his silence, the solicitor told him to try St. Ignatius' County Home. That's where they have the registry office for your side of the County these days, he said, so you should be able to get both certificates there. It's on the Killygordon road coming out of Ballyfinn, not the Letterkenny road, now. You go on away and pass the new fire station, and then you'll see it up on your left. Can't miss it. They needed a coroners' report due to the sudden nature of your father's death, but you should be able to obtain a copy of some kind, for sure.

They don't know how he died?

Not officially, said the solicitor. It's not really my place to say, but I believe it was a heart attack. You would need to speak to his doctor or the coroner about that.

Who found him, do you know?

I believe it was a neighbour, but again, I only have patchy information on those details.

Christ, he said, I'm not sure where to start, after all this.

I do sympathise, said the solicitor. It's awfully sad that these administrative burdens come on top of grieving and suffering the loss of a loved one, said the solicitor.

He took the envelopes and stood up to shake the solicitor's hand.

The high-backed executive chair gave out a startled fart as the solicitor rose quickly to meet the outstretched hand. My sincere condolences on your loss, said the solicitor.

I'll be in touch, he said.

ANDREA CARO

The Fair

Synopsis

SEAN and VITA's lives are changed forever when 'The Fair' comes to town in this sprawling literary romance. Weaving together deep prejudice, family secrets and the frailty of love, the novel explores the illusory nature of freedom and what it really means to be free.

Quiet and unassuming, Sean is rich and about to embark on a degree he didn't choose for a career he doesn't want. Beneath the veneer of his perfect, suburban family life, everything is quietly disintegrating. Bright and opinionated, Vita has only ever known life on the road. As the daughter of the fairground owner, she feels trapped within the insular life of the fair and dreams of educating herself to escape. After a chance encounter brings Sean and Vita together, events in their lives conspire to draw them ever closer and they find themselves falling in love with the freedom the other represents. Amidst the heady excesses of summer nights and the charged hedonism of the fair, this is a fated love story between two people whose lives are worlds apart.

Set against a background of political upheaval in mid-eighties London, 'The Fair' spins classic themes of class, deception and sexuality to form the heart of this exploration of love, loyalty and what happens when the fun is finally over.

1. Memory

It was the crash of the lights through the trees on the Castle Road he would always remember. A brilliant blue that beckoned him into the tree-ringed scorched-grass meadows, to the Fair. Sean remembered being five or six and walking that road with his parents. The hot pavement damp from rain, bitumen tar through woodsmoke. A billowing swag of sound would echo far along the tree-lined avenue, the still summer air carrying wafts of hot stale oil, vinegared chips and burger meat patties. Sean would hurry to keep up on scar-scuffed knees, browned from hot Summer gardens. He'd beg his mother to let him have a treat, just one stick of sticky spun sugar from the rim encrusted silver drum. She would tell Sean not to drag his feet, that they would have to see. Then his father would lift him high onto his shoulders above the jostling heads of the crowd. Sean would watch as the blue of the sign emerged in a halo of stellar light, rapt by a promise of something uncommonly rare through the canopies of Summer trees.

2. Sean

He was late to meet Jerry, zig-zagging his way through the crowds along the avenue. As he drew nearer, the beating thud of rhythm and noise came at him through the heat. A low bass hum of generator drone, the deranged Wurlitzer of the carousel. Sean looked ahead to the high domed roof that rose above the crowns of the trees and wondered if Helter Skelters were always red. He could make out the corkscrew turns of its helix, lit by dozens of oily yellow bulbs that snaked towards the crowds on the ground beneath. Miniature figures slid down the slide at speed like coloured marbles. It reminded him of the girl in his art class who'd painted strange fairground scenes. Ferris wheels with monkey headed passengers, Helter Skelters with snake-infested sacks. Huge paintings, sometimes 7ft tall. The girl's name was Rachel and she'd been sharp-witted and sullen, Sean one of only two boys in a class of twenty-four girls. She wore paint-spattered boilersuits and had multiple piercings and he'd found her disregard for him wildly attractive. He'd spent that term toying with telling his parents he wanted to go to art school and become a photographer.

He breathed into a cupped hand, then pulled a stick of gum from his jeans, finding the fiver he'd meant to get changed at the kiosk. He spotted the boys standing by the entrance gates, Jerry's ginger mullet a bright beacon above the crowds. His lanky frame stooped, gesturing wildly at Simon who stood laughing, tight t-shirt stretched to bursting over scrum-half arms.

'Bill's not coming. He busted his Dad's car.'

'Shit.'

'I know.'

They walked through the large iron gates and headed straight for the bumper cars. Crowds of people jostled through the late sunlit evening, past brightly coloured bulbs of fairground signage. Sound waves ricocheted through avenues of rides, doppler shifting as each step brought harmony and dissonance. Tinny nasal pop fought jangling electric overdrive, beneath it all a pulsing dub bass that beat inside your chest. A grinning kid walked past, dwarfed by a giant blue Smurf he'd won, train-track brace smile lit by hundreds of coloured lights. Sean reached for the camera that hung from his neck to take a shot before remembering he had yet to load the film he'd stuffed into his camera bag. He turned back to see Jerry and Simon already climbing into the dodgem cars, gripping the immobilised steering wheels and trying to move them from side to side like little kids. A boy in a turquoise, nylon shell-suit took their coins as the claxon sounded and the cars jumped to life. Sean reached the low metal steps just in time to see Jerry accelerating at Simon who turned his wheel into a spin, heading straight for a pair of screaming girls whose feigned outrage goaded him on. There ensued a chase as the girls chased Simon and Simon chased them and Jerry came crashing into Simon, all three cars slamming sideways, slaloming into the barriers.

'I've gotta load this.' Sean shouted, pointing to his camera. Over the claxons and the music and the screaming laughter, none of them heard him. He pushed his way past the mass of people that stood and queued or milled around, past the stalls selling sentry lines of blood red toffee apples and honeycomb pocked like pumice rock.

'Can I go around the back to load this?' he asked the woman at the change kiosk, gesturing to his camera as she counted out his change.

'Sorry. Private.' She spoke without looking up, beckoning to the girls behind him to step forward.

He waited until she was distracted then ducked beneath the rail around the back of the kiosk. He knelt down on crisp parched grass and opened up the case of his camera, laying it down to shield it from the last dying flares of sunlight. He pulled the leader from the cannister, secured it to the spindle and then closed the camera back and began to wind, clicking the shutter and then winding it on until the first frame was ready. Pressed to his eye he aimed the lens upwards, framing the vastness of the big wheel against the cobalt brightness of the sky. But as his finger pushed the button someone stepped into the frame, ruining the shot at the last minute.

'You're not supposed to be here.'

Sean looked up at the girl looking down at him, backlit by the flare of rays departing the sky.

'I needed shade.'

'You don't need shade.'

'Yeah I do. I'm trying to load my film. See?' he held up his camera

'You don't need shade.'

'You do when you load film into a camera.'

'Not in this evening light you don't.'

Sean squinted up at the girl but couldn't make out her features. A halo of hair hung wild about her face, gold hoops hanging just beneath the curls.

'So, you'll have to move. It's private.'

'Alright, I'm done anyway. Sorry.'

The girl turned to leave as Sean rose from the ground, slinging the camera over his shoulder. He watched her as she walked away, jeans tucked into cowboy boots, paint spattered workman's belt slung low over her hips. She twisted her hair into a knot of curls and was gone behind a trailer. Sean ducked back beneath the rail and walked across the fairground to the dodgems, finding them silently awaiting new drivers. From the steps he scanned the crowds, taking a picture of a bloke taking aim at a bullseye, then a kid doing wheelies on his yellow wheeled burner bike. His belly grumbled loudly as hot chip fat wafted through the warm night. A tap came on his shoulder and made him jump.

'Hey Sean!'

'Hey Deborah.'

'Simon's meeting you right?'

'Jerry and Simon yeah. They were on the dodgems. I went to –'

'– did you hear about Bill's Dad's car? He was supposed to drive me to Brighton.'

'Yeah, I heard'

The girls behind Deborah giggled as Sean checked his watch.

'We'll help you find them, won't we girls?'

Deborah linked her arm through Sean's as fifteen wound loops of fake pearls dug into his forearm. Fumes of solvent hairspray caught in the back of his throat. They walked past a chubby punk, his baby-face out of kilter with his glue hard mohawk, as beside him a massive ghetto blaster blared out the Clash.

'Bet you're feeling chuffed, Jerry told us you smashed your grades. Gonna be a hot shot city boy with a Porsche?'

'Not really.'

Deborah laughed, as an orb of bubble-gum grew from her mouth, bursting to a flaccid film across her lips. They spotted Simon in the crowd as Deborah slipped Sean's grip, leaving little half-moon imprints from her plastic pearls across his wrist as she called to Jerry.

'Hey Jerry! How's your creepy arm?'

'Hey Deborah.'

All three girls broke into hysterical laughter. Jerry hadn't lived down last year's gossip, the clumsy cinema double date when he'd over-reached the shoulders of the girl he'd taken and accidentally placed his hand on her best friend's chest. No amount of pleading explanation would convince either of the girls it had been a mistake. They'd made damned sure everyone knew about Jerry's arm and there wasn't a girl who didn't know him now as *creepy Jerry*.

Sean stood in line with the others, watching the steady stream of ghost train cars burst at speed through the flip-flap doors, relieved that Deborah had swapped his arm for Simon's. A pair of punks with matching tangerine mohawks emerged nodding both their heads in approval. Thirty seconds later they were followed by an old couple having the time of their lives. Their faces a topography of tightly packed contours, wrinkles fanning out from their eyes and mouths. The old girl sported a spectacular black bouffant wig that matched the replacement kohl black eyebrows she'd drawn on. Behind them, a couple came out snogging and Sean recognised the girl from his street. His mother knew her mother, she was some kind of sports champion, hockey possibly or was it la crosse? They'd played a game of tennis once at his mother's insistence in which she'd mercilessly thrashed him. He remembered how she'd shaken his hand at the net like a Wimbledon pro.

He moved up in the queue as Deborah and Simon climbed into an empty car and began trundling slowly forwards. Deborah began screaming even before the double doors swung open and swallowed them both whole, the speakers crackling and spitting *Let's Go Crazy* overhead. Deborah's friends took the next car as Sean and Jerry climbed into the one behind squashing themselves in. Their knees were thrust into their chests as they sat, their bodies too big for the small studded metal seats. It reminded Sean of his Dad and how they always used to ride the ghost train together, his young legs next to his father's which would be squashed and bent double just like his were now. He would try to chat to Sean over his laughing screams, but he could never hear what it was his Dad was saying.

After the ghost train, Sean felt queasy with hunger and left the others queuing for the Meteorite. The fair was heaving with people now drunk or hungry, winning or losing. Sean had always loved to disappear amongst the roiling swell of fractious energy, the air charged with a million colliding particles, punch ups, adrenalin, elicit encounters. The pickpockets, the drunk kids, all the fun of the fair in the effervescent buzz of noise and light and heat. He got himself some food and stood eating at one of the tall metal tables, dipping vinegared chips into ketchup. At the arcade opposite a kid was winning at Asteroids, his friends crowding round to share his victory.

Next door stood the hook-a-duck stall, its painted circular roof the red and yellow stripes of a circus big top. Prizes hung from the roof, fluffy pastel elephants, packets of candy cigarettes and bags and bags of goldfish. They hung there, beautiful and gape-mouthed in their distended bags of water, bulging creases shot through with refracted light. Two young boys were hooking ducks while their mother stood next to them, fishing endless coins from inside her purse. The girl running the stall turned around and Sean instantly recognised the hair, the dark wild curls. He watched as she held out a hand to the mother to take more coins, gesturing to the littlest boy then whispering in his ear. Then she stood next to the floating ducks and trapped one with her hooked rod so the little kid could finally catch one of them. Sean watched the relieved mother thank the girl as she lifted down a goldfish and handed it to the beaming kid.

They walked away and Sean watched as the girl caught her hair and twisted it into a bun again, curls escaping at all angles. Then a blonde-haired man came over, wiry arms tattooed and fighter pilot aviators covering his eyes. He and the girl talked for a while looking around them, the girl nodding as he spoke and gesturing. She laughed out loud at something and then as the man left, she looked directly over to where Sean stood looking at her. He looked down to his half-eaten chips and spent a good minute pushing one around and around the polystyrene plate. When he looked back up again the girl's back was turned, taking money from a father and handing a little girl a hooking rod.

'Found ya!' Jerry grabbed Sean's shoulders from behind

'Jesus, man!'

'Come on Sean, you stuffed your face enough?'

Jerry nicked a chip as the others arrived behind him, Deborah stepping forward and ruffling Sean's hair.

'I could have done with you back there, I thought this one was gonna throw up.' she gestured towards Simon, all colour drained from his face.

'Want some?' Jerry waved a flaccid chip in the air at Simon, who sat down heavily on the grass with his knees up. One of Deborah's friends joined him on the ground, sitting close beside and rubbing his shoulders in sympathy.

Sean left the rest of the chips to Jerry and they all headed off, past the hook-a-duck towards the shooting gallery. As they passed by, Sean looked over to the girl standing beneath prismed bags of goldfish as the tracking lines of lights lit the top of her head.

Meat

Synopsis

Meat *is a speculative novel, a* Brave New World *for the XR generation. Fifty years after the green revolution people live sustainable lives in settlements, directed by the Committee under a mysterious Moderator. The farms have been liberated and meat is literally murder. But this idyllic society is not cost free. After a succession of hard winters, human- and animal-beings face starvation.*

Robert keeps the village's two ancient wind turbs like his father who plunged to his death ten years before. He salvages dead rabbits to eat and trade with an illegal meaterer for medicine for his mother. For this, he risks a reputedly terrible fate. After helping the village cover up a series of gruesome animal murders and following a riot over taxes, Robert is accused of murdering a cow by his brother and a village elder. But what is the Moderator's connection to Robert's fate? And is his strange love of 'his' wolves just a little bit un-revolutionary?

Bel is a Woman: healer, mind-seer, member of the elite. She admired the Moderator but is now troubled. Her friend and co Woman Squirrel ran away. Guilt-stricken for failing to see something was wrong, she suspects the Moderator. An unknown prisoner has been brought in for trial at the fiftieth anniversary celebrations. At first, she refuses to help him (Robert). Then she discovers something implicating the Moderator in Squirrel's disappearance and changes her mind, hoping Robert will help her in turn. She must find out what really happened in the village before Robert's trial or he will be convicted and fed to the Moderator's wolves, an apt end for an animal murderer. Finally, she must face the worst question of all: what happened to her friend.

Great Reckoning, Year 50 [GR:50]: Feb 25
The Cow & the Dragon

THE ONE-EYED COW has attitude. She straddles the moor path like an old-time farmer surveying her acres, making snatches at the frozen ground then lifting her head to out-stare the storm. In the lowland forests there are bears and wolves. Up here, the cow-being is the Alpha. Knock-kneed, bow-backed, the sores on her patched hide are exposed like the lichen that clings to rocks.

Once or twice she lashes her tail jauntily, as if beset by fly-beings even in February when they are still maggots snug-down in rotted leaves and shit lying in wait for spring. A spring this cow will not see.

For now, she is eyeing the shape of a boy-being that stands in her path. Cold and hungry, he regrets following his neighbour Robert who is the keeper of the wind towers. Beaten by his lump of a sister again, he was angry with her and his Mam and Dad and the baby and even the cat-being. Now he is beginning to think there are worse things. He has tripped and fallen into something both crisp and soft, dung from the herds. It's all over his clothes. His Mam will kill him.

'Move yous-self!' he whispers at the cow. If she hears, she gives no sign. She regards him as she would a clump of grass only less important. He has heard terrible things about cows. He is glad the herds have kept away this winter. They trample crops. They destroy things. Starved-looking or not they can kill a man- or a boy-being. He knows of at least one boy died that way.

Some believe cows can see in the dark. No-one can say for sure. Since the farms were liberated, human-beings tend to avoid them as no-use-nor-ornament. Head down it is true her range of vision is impeccable on her good side. Head-up, no better than the average human-being's. But she can hear. The comforting lowing of the fractured herd higher up the moor and the scream of the gale through the gorse.

Suddenly she blinks and bellows. The boy steps back abruptly and falls in a hole where bracken hides him. She pauses in mid-chew, drooling. Lowers her head. Some sound or smell disturbs her, a flicker of herd memory from the dark destroying times. She emits another uneasy bellow. A qualified warning. Waits, maimed vision considering singularly every squat shape, shrub, bramble, splayed bracken. All seems familiar and good.

Whatever caused alarm is forgotten. With a hostile toss, as if protesting the inconvenience, she lifts her head once more and carries on chewing. Kneeling in the hollow, the boy witnesses a sleek form surge along the path, its ascending roar blending with the wind. Cowering, he remembers his sister's stories about dragons. And he has heard his Mam and Dad talking in the middle of the night about the dead beings, too.

The cow widens her eyes, startled, but does not have any time left to drop her big head. The luminescent eyes blind and terrify her. There is a blur of ferocious, continuous momentum, a flash of silver, a predatory screech and the roaring beast hits her flank. The boy feels it in his bones. The cow utters a strange, high-pitched bleat. It is her last.

31

The monster stops further along the path growling, smoke pouring from its front. It crouches there, its red eyes narrow and mean. As the boy waits cringing, he sees under the moonlight a man-being climb out of the beast's belly. The long pale face under a hood looks sad. The man walks slowly towards the cow. As he does so, the moon goes in and the boy scrambles out of the hollow, lifts up his legs and runs for his life, his screams masked by the fierce wind.

Further off, he slows panting for breath and peers back. The poor cow is still standing but something is wrong. Her left leg sticks out all funny and she lolls to one side. There is a kind of blackness where her jaw was that gives her a surprised look. One of her horns is dangling. As the boy watches, she topples and falls on her side, her patches quivering in the moonlight.

The man looks at the fallen cow. There is the glint of something shiny in his hand. And as he bends over the cow, his face catches the moonlight. For a split second the boy sees him.

He runs screaming and does not stop till he gets back home to a row of cottages overlooking the moor.

GR:50: Feb 15
The Thirteen

THE BURIAL PARTY are getting plastered when the twelve Committee members pass Miller's cottage. A collective shudder – like a coming sickness – grips them.

'Well, there wes are then. They's here.' Robert slurps his drink. The brew warms his belly but leaves the rest of him cold. He shivers beside the remains of the fire, its plum-and-ash colours flickering over five blurred and troubled faces. The green robes process slowly by the window.

'They's here all right,' says the host, drawing in breath, which sounds loud in the silence. Their heads pivot to Miller's work spade propped against the wall in a corner. Chunks of drying mud cling to its blade, brown and blood reddish.

'Why did theys have to come tonight? Int as if theys can be rehearsing in dark,' says Miller. 'Why? This day of all?'

No-being replies. They gawk at the column of revolutionary officials. The electrics went off for curfew and there are no soy candles, so they sit in the dark. The turbs only support so much use. Tonight, Robert thinks, it might be a good thing. Not to be seen.

He passes a hand over his mouth, to stop he-self blurting out the panic in his mind; what they all must be feeling but no-being says. And it were all at Sangstam's behest – yet he is conveniently absent, as he were the other times too.

'Odd doings.' Miller's voice, sharp and a bit slurred from the bramble wine, almost breaks the greasy film of fear. They stir and rub their backs, aching from digging frozen ground, and Miller passes round the jug. His hand tremors - some of his brew splashes out. They stare like eye-wide idiots at the deep red splatters until Miller's daughter takes a cloth and erases the spills with a couple of swipes of her hand.

Only old Clifford seems not to notice the kerfuffle. He's still at the window, as if held there by magic.

'Int as if wes not seen Badger-beings 'for,' Miller says.

'But never all twelve on them together,' Robert says.

'And then, only when tax is due,' Moxon of the Heap adds.

'We had taxes in my day too,' Clifford mutters. 'Quiet. I's counting.' Moxon makes a gesture as if to say the old man's losing it at last.

Robert goes to stand next to Clifford at the window. 'Badgers' is a good nickname for them, he thinks. The Committee's eyes are narrowed on Sangstam Sangstam's house in the Square. The senior Alder has got one of his speeches prepared. So that'll be a treat! The streaming torch carried by Sangstam's son silvers the long white streaks in the Committee's flowing locks. Seen together, they look exactly like twelve identical badgers.

'Moderator among them?' asks Moxon, trying to sound casual. His voice, hoarse from the wine, gives him away.

Robert peers out. A few villagers hover like ghosts in the Committee's passing but the youngs in the crowd are over-excited. Probably hoping for a glimpse.

'No sign of any-being that could be he,' he says, glad folk seem to be wrong about that. A rumour went round the Moderator he-self was overseeing preparations for this year's Howling. What he looks like, no-being knows? He has not been seen in the village for many years.

He shudders. Is even Sangstam trembling as he prepares for his speeching? Sangstam should have reported it, but he told them they'd have all got blamed. Whole settlements have been flattened for less. And now, they'll be in worse trouble if they're found out.

Behind the Badgers the Women pass by, their strangeness hidden beneath their hoods and cloaks.

Robert swills the sticky blackness round in his beaker, losing his taste for it. Miller's famous bramble cannot burn away the oily tang at the back of his throat from this afternoon's work.

33

Clifford by the window looks as if he's been turned to rock. The rest stare at their fingers. Right now, holding the Howling nearby seems less like a great honour, more like a curse.

Clifford strains his gobble-chuck neck to not lose sight of the Committee as they vanish into the Square. He mutters something.

'Eh?' asks Miller. 'Close shutters, will yous.' Clifford ignores him.

The host gives him a prod. 'Drink yous wine, 'for yous spill it. Yous an Alder, anyhow. Why int yous out there with them?'

The old man blinks at Miller. 'There int twelve.'

For a minute the tension beats like a heart in the room. Even the fire has gone out. In its last embers, Clifford's ancient eyes glow.

'Not twelve. Thirteen.'

'What do yous mean, not twelve?' Miller says. 'There's always been twelve buggers. 'Twelve to administer, twelve to protect'.'

Clifford gives a raspy laugh. 'That'd make twenty-four.'

'No, what it means is –'

Robert strains his eyes. He's learnt to count a bit. It seems like twelve to him but it's hard to count moving figures in the swirling dark.

'There's thirteen,' Old Clifford repeats as if it matters.

Miller, catching the old man's excitement, squints out then uses his chunky fingers. 'Twelve.' He sounds doubtful.

'It's thirteen,' Clifford insists.

Robert can hear their breathing, paused. Unless the old man has finally lost his mind, they all know he must be right. He used to be a school-teacher before the Great Reckoning. Is it important? They might mock and call him chat-gob, but Clifford usually has a reason.

'All right, there's thirteen, if it'll shut yous up,' Moxon says. 'More wine, will yous, Miller?'

Clifford doesn't say anything. His eyes gleam angrily.

With a sinking heart, Robert asks, 'So who's the thirteenth?'

'The Moderator, 'course.'

Robert feels his flesh crinkle and a damp sensation fold over him. The Committee were a named fear. What he feels now is nameless. Like most of the villagers, he's never met the Moderator. Years ago, before he were Moderator, he helped re-forest the land and re-wild the forests, it's said. Why they'd want to put beings like bears where they weren't before, that can kill you with a swipe of the hand, he doesn't know, but he's ignorant. It must have been a good thing or why would it have been done?

The silence grows. It has awe in it as well as fear.

'So yous reckon the Moderator's here, Cliff?' chimes up Miller's daughter. 'Then I's want to see this.'

Before they can stop her the girl surges out into the street and intoxed they blunder after her, forgetting fear. Besides, as Moxon hisses, they're as safe outdoors as in. Or nowhere. But Robert, coming last, feels like a lump of ice has got wedged under his ribs.

The Square has filled up with villagers. A man-being stands beside Sangstam on a makeshift platform. When the Alder finishes his oratoricals and the man steps forward, a cheer goes up. That alone makes him different from the Committee, who are tolerated, if they must be, with silence. Though of course, the cheer might be because Sangstam stopped talking.

'That's he,' murmurs Clifford. The old man's voice quivers and is too loud.

'Primos into parus. They all dress same. Show they's equal.'

Even without seeing his face, Robert can tell this is not an ordinary Badger. Though what the difference is, is hard to say. His hair and clothes are the same. The man turns his head slightly, as if catching his thoughts. It is a long, sad face. The tall, spare body exudes authority and something Robert does not know the word for. Anyhow, it makes him sorry for the evil he has done.

Clifford lowers his voice. 'I met he's father once. That were before he went south – Weren't like these. Didn't go in for all this dressing up. Dressed like a normal man.' Robert glances at the old man, wondering what he's talking about.

The Moderator's voice is high-pitched when he speaks, which is at first shocking and makes you want to laugh. But then he settles into his words and it is as if all other voices are at fault. It is a voice made from streams and rainbows.

'Spring is near, let nature provide. This is the power and achievement of our great Revolution. Let the sun warm you and the earth feed you. Do not despoil the earth.'

When he chastises them about illegal bracken burning, he sounds almost kind – like a mam chastising a young, who, because young, does not understand. It is like he is saying, when you are a grown you will be as wise as I am.

A cold easterly blowing through the Square makes Robert shudder and fold his arms, but the crowd do not seem to notice.

'It is a long while since I last came to your village, but it has a place in my heart. I spent several happy days here once, in my youth.' He smiles. Like a man in torment, Robert thinks.

'This settlement is privileged to be the venue for the Fiftieth Anniversary Howling, chosen from all the settlements in the region. Fifty years ago, in what you know as the Great Reckoning, we wrested Mother Earth from the hands of her exploiters ….'

The spidery fingers make patterns in the air as he talks.

Then the Moderator praises the village's diligence in the maintenance of the turbs. As if they all did it.

When he finishes, the Women start up with their chants. All the songs begin and end, *Thank you, O Earth* or similar.

Beside him, Old Clifford stamps his feet, still muttering about the past.

'You's all right, Cliff?'

'Bit cold.'

'Yous should go home.'

Suddenly, the Moderator looks at him. Him. Robert. Not any-being else. His lips twitch into a smile. And Robert feels the blood drain from his face.

SAM CHRISTIE

Compass

Synopsis

In a world where forgiveness is becoming a thing of the past, all that remains is retribution.

Bilal Aldhamook *is stuck on a rooftop near the old city of Mosul with his comrade* **Anwar***. It's 2017 and the allied Special Forces, the Iraqi army and the Kurds are retaking the city. Neither of these young British Jihadis wants to be a martyr anymore, if they ever did. As the fighting intensifies the two boys have one way out; to pretend to be civilians and creep away. Bilal manages to get out during the fierce fighting but Anwar is killed. Bilal is interrogated and returns to the UK to face the music.*

Three thousand miles away in a small village in mid Wales, **Pete Lewis** *is standing outside the front of his house surrounded by his possessions. He's committed the ultimate sin and in a rage has pushed his girlfriend* **Jen** *into a kitchen unit; arguably with some justification. It seems there's no way back from this, so Pete decides to escape for a while. He goes on a long walk.*

Two days into the wild walk, Pete is caught in a heavy storm and decides to take shelter in a remote bothy in the hills. When he arrives he is not alone; two far right activists are there already. Pete discovers to his horror that these two people, **Ryan** *and* **Suzi***, have kidnapped* **Bilal** *and plan to behead him on camera in an eye for an eye style stunt. Pete must find a way to rescue Bilal and after a very tense night finally manages to knock out the couple and make a run for it. Bilal refuses to go to the police and instead just wants a Coca Cola.*

Compass
Chapter 1

From the rooftop position the city looked as if its streets were moving and shape-shifting in real time. It wasn't due to the residents, scurrying between bombed out shop fronts that made it seem that way; it was the streets themselves that seemed to be constantly changing their physical reality. Hunger or heat might have played some part, possibly inducing a

37

mild hallucination, but to Bilal the streets looked like the constantly shifting maze he'd once seen in a film. Up on the top of the old office building it was possible to see far into the distance, at least in one direction, and from here it was clear that a combination of airstrikes and skirmishes had shifted rubble, burned out cars and left holes where the tarmac once was. This movement was a city in its final death throes. Daily, even hourly, the situation changed and not just physically. The areas where it was possible to move safely had narrowed further and further until more crushing layers of fear crept into the men in the hollowed out buildings in and around the old city. It was possible to map out the battle onto the grim vista by transposing the sporadic reports, shouted in Arabic, from the Motorola handset lying next to Bilal that crackled into life every so often making his heart beat a little faster. Predominantly the news on the airwaves was grim, though luckily for Bilal the true nature of it was softened slightly because his Arabic wasn't good enough to immediately pick up on the numbers of dead or the rough guesses about when the next coalition force's push might start. He understood the basics however, and had come to know Mosul well enough to recognise the names of the areas that had fallen: Al Bakr, Ilam, Tamim, the Nineveh Ruins. The list went on and on relentlessly and charted a slow and circuitous route to his comrades, and therefore his own, probable death in the remains of the old city. Having a good imagination Bilal often shuddered when he could no longer block the vision of his bloodied body, twisted on rubble and sand, from his mind. He had stopped wishing to be a martyr many months ago if he'd ever really wanted to be one at all.

This city-wide movement he perceived from the roof reminded him of his home, Southampton, in a small way. Not much of a city, a rather forgotten place in the very south of England. Big, but sort of pointless. It was best known for the cruise ships and, at least at one time, for having the biggest shopping centre in Europe. He could never work out what people did there, but they must have done something as almost everyone seemed to have a big German car and the houses cost lots of money. In Southampton, just like here, there were plenty of places that he couldn't go; risks that could be serious. If he passed the wrong group of lads at best he'd be called 'Raghead' or 'Paki', at worst he'd get punched or even stabbed. Back there it was better to remain in the same area as much as possible to minimise the danger. Here in Mosul, at least now, there was a similar claustrophobia that came from ever present risk. At least back in the UK, those risks didn't seem to be looking for him, they were just there and after a while, even the surprising, nasty encounters that came out of the blue in supermarkets or on the street became predictable and therefore manageable. He remembered his A-Level sociology teacher, Mr Moon, telling the class about these weird French guys in Paris in the sixties who just got drunk and walked around the city. Sometimes they used the maps of other cities to complicate the routes, sometimes they just crawled from bar to bar. Mr Moon, a thin, carefully spoken and gentle man, explained that their objective was really a sort of revolution: by walking around in this way, they were going against the purpose for which the city was designed. He said that the city had been built to serve the French military and its wide streets and geometric arrangement were made that way to provide corridors for the marching army in case of revolution. Rather than pick up guns – these madmen just walked – bending the expectations of the grids and blocks, defying the rules gently, thoughtfully and spent the evenings writing about how it all felt. They too bent cities out of shape, but in their wake they left nothing but tuts of disapproval. Mr Moon had said these people were like the skateboarders by Southampton Guildhall, or the free runners that did those amazing stunts on the cantilevered chins of buildings or the walls and staircases outside the station. Same thing. Bilal couldn't remember the name the French guys gave themselves, but he remembered how he'd longed to join in with those free runners and how the whole concept made sense to him.

Of course, for the French in Paris back then, this walking revolution in some ways was a good old joke or some sort of means of expression. But here when you saw a woman clutching a baby, sprinting fast over rough ground which was maybe once a car park, or through the doorway of a bombed out police station hunched as low as possible, it wasn't a choice or any sort of statement. Here you took a left by the wheelie bin with the legs sticking out, a bin you could smell long before you saw it. Here you could map the whole place on the basis of the bodies that lay around. His comrades and him did use the bodies as geographical landmarks, mostly due to the indelible scars they left on the memory. They all knew where 'Kurdish pants' was. He was lying on a black stain in the road, with half of his rotting body on the high curb, his burnt papery head sporting a gaping hole. Take a left after 'Kurdish pants', run like fuck down sniper alley and once you get to 'desert boots' – just legs and a torso – you were close to the second insurgent position and a small amount of safety. In fact there were plenty of Frenchmen here stalking around the city: though these were not drunk revolutionaries, but lean, hard-eyed soldiers picking their way quietly through the rubble with deliberate movements that only came with tough, relentless training. Through his rifle scope he could easily tell these men, who wore pleasing green uniforms and carried extremely hi-tech kit. It was easy to tell them from the Peshmerga

(Kurds), the Iraqis and the other Joint Task Force Special Forces that skulked in the shadows. They all wore skull face ski masks too and that scared Bilal and his friends as it was supposed to. There was an old film he'd seen as a kid where these skeletons danced with swords and shields and it had terrified Bilal, sending him hiding behind the sofa, much to the amusement of his brothers. In one sense when he saw the French, Bilal wanted to run outside and hold up his hands. He wanted them to save him too, not just the Iraqi civilians who had endured all this. The French acted like adults and adults never killed children, so now that he was afraid, he wanted them to pick him up, with their reassuring smell of sweat and take him away. The trouble was he knew, as did everyone else, that their decision to come here and participate in all this had rendered them adults too; on the same playing field as the various soldiers that wanted them dead. He also knew that it was these French soldiers that had been sent to kill the insurgents, especially French citizens that had chosen to wage Jihad, even if they were surrendering. He doubted being English would make much difference to a world's desire for him to no longer exist; now, as always, Bilal was an outsider. Now, as the corner had already been turned, he couldn't change his mind and say sorry.

The sounds tended to unnerve him the most. Where he lay, under the small wall at the edge of the rooftop, the big boxy air conditioners would bang and start whirring whenever the electricity supply would briefly come back on, giving him a sudden burst of adrenaline that took too long to dissipate. These air-con units made him feel very far from home as there was no need for these in Southampton. He remembered the wet glistening pavements of London Road and pined for the squish of his wet trainers and that smell that seemed to puff out from the big trees on the common in the rain. Mosul was full of the sounds of a war-torn city and now, in the late stages of the allied campaign to take it back, they were all a direct threat to him and his friends. There was the constant, distant crack of small arms fire. He'd learnt to tell the difference between an AK47 and a Colt M4, a difference that mattered since one was the weapon they carried, but the other, with its neat staccato snap, almost always belonged to the enemy. The booms and thumps were more worrying, but after some time getting used to them, they all knew that as long as those sounds stayed outside a very specific acoustic boundary they were no problem. Every so often that boundary line was crossed and it always made the boy's eyes wider and tensed their bodies for them. Planes were horrifying. As a kid he remembered how excited he'd be if he saw a military plane skimming the treetops of the Hampshire countryside or a fat helicopter thudding along importantly, but now those sounds were sounds from hell.

The F15s were always above them, they became the bass section to the orchestral ensemble of this desert war, rumbling in the stratosphere until some coded order sent them down to a target below. They knew an attack was imminent when this constant rumbling would start to break up and then suddenly surge forth like thunder, which would then twist into a roar until the ground shook after a laser bomb crunched onto its target, In'shallah, far in the distance. They lived in permanent fear of a laser guided bomb delivered by a sweet-smelling American pilot.

'I want a coke bro.' It was Anwar, a fellow British fighter slumped down at the other edge of the roof. He didn't seem anywhere near as anxious as Bilal. Anwar was a skinny delinquent from Brighton who always wanted something. He was scrolling on his phone and leaning languidly against the low wall. Impossibly he had the bored expression of a teenager splayed out on a fat sofa watching Netflix. Chances were that it was an act. No-one was genuinely calm here now.

'Coke is Haram' Bilal replied, knowing where the conversation was going to lead.

'Haram! Fuck off man, coke is a drink bro. It's just a drink.' Anwar reached for the little dirty copy of the Qu'ran he always kept by his side. 'Anyway brother, I got the last stuff. I'm going to see in here if coke is haram. Like, as if coke is haram, fuck's sake.'

'Anwar, leave the Qu'ran. How do you think the holy book is going to tell you that? Excuse me Mohammad, but any chance I can have a coke? Like, what's a coke?'

'It's all about finding out something *like* that. Like, could it be haram if it was in a different time? Maybe like some lime drink or whatever. *Interpretation* man.'

Bilal peered over the wall to check the street below. For now there was no one around and even the sounds of the fighting had receded a little. 'There's no interpretation going on here Anwar.'

'Come on bro, how long have we been here for? It's been like four hours man. It's mad hot.' Anwar squirmed on the stony concrete surface, his desert boots improbably large and jutting out from his long, thin legs.

'It's always mad hot. Mate, you've been here a year.' Bilal liked him, he liked his nonchalant attitude. He could see that the hard life Anwar must have lead before coming to the Middle East had prepared him perfectly. While Anwar didn't talk much about home, Bilal had picked up a lot in the cracks of their banter. He knew he hadn't had it half as hard as Anwar back in the UK.

'You know where to go man. Just go down to the Chechen and ask him for two cokes and some Lay's. You're scared of the Chechen innit?'

41

Anwar smirked. Anwar seemed to have less fear and Bilal wondered how much of that was a version of 'fuck it' and how much was a strong belief in God and all the stuff they'd been told. Anwar had faith, but it resembled the faith a child had in Santa Claus.

'Yeah, I'm sacred of him, because he's an animal. Like a proper fucking nutter.'

'We're brothers, muqatil, brothers. He's only gonna chop your head off if you're a kuffir. I think he likes you anyway. He's always watching you!' Anwar giggled childishly.

'Okay, okay. Coke – the drink – is not haram, you're haram.' Bilal shifted on the crunchy ground and prepared to get into a crouch to make an assessment of the street he'd have to cross to get to the Chechen.

Bilal was right to be scared of the Chechen. He would have been right to be scared of all of them. They were the battle-hardened, leathery fighters that had led most of the campaigns in this country or Syria in the near past. Everyone feared them, with their lethal combination of Slavic pragmatism, hard fought skill and unwavering faith. It was known, through radio interceptions, that even the Special Forces hard-nuts were at the very least wary of the Chechens and a few had been killed by them. You make monstrous soldiers by first creating the rock of oppression, indignity and revenge; then carve the shape of murderous efficiency. Not only did the Chechens have all that, they had Allah and the promises given to martyrs.

TRACY COOK

Room for Doubt

Synopsis
After waking naked in a hotel room after a girls' night, with no idea where she is, a mum hides what's happened to protect her family, but her life unravels until she risks losing everything. Women's fiction influenced by Apple Tree Yard *and* Queenie.

Nina Bradley has spent a lifetime controlling her feelings. She's held it all together since she was fifteen, when her brother died and her parents gave up.

Now Nina's married to Adam, a mum of two and a PR crisis manager. She's also supporting her mother through cancer and steering daughter Molly through gym competitions. Whether you need a press campaign or an ironed shirt, she's your woman.

What she can't do, is ask for help.

But when Nina goes on a night out, she's faced with a crisis even she can't control. It threatens to destroy her. She wakes the next morning in a hotel room with no idea where she is, or how she got there.

She's been raped. Distraught, she is terrified the police will raise the question of consent. And worse, what about Adam? She cheated on him once, a mistake, years before. Will he believe her now?

To protect her family, Nina takes the only way out she's ever known and the only way she can control: denial. She lies to Adam, her family and her boss. Most of all, she lies to herself.

But she cannot forget her devastating secret. Triggered by a sexual harassment case at work and a huge row with Adam, she makes a disastrous mistake and risks losing Adam, the children and her job.

When teenage Molly is assaulted at a party, Nina is forced to choose between her secret and her family. Will she finally find the strength to ask for help?

Chapter One

I knew before I even opened my eyes that something was wrong.

The pillow smelt of unfamiliar washing powder, the cotton too crisp. A cold draught blew across my shoulder. My toe caught in a too heavy duvet.

My throat scraped raw, the metallic taste in my mouth bitter, as if I'd sucked a coin all night. I stirred and iron bands gripped my head.

'Adam,' I croaked. My lips ached, shaping the words. 'Can you get me some water?'

Silence.

'Adam?' I tried again. 'Water?'

My temples throbbed. Christ, how much had I drunk last night?

I rubbed my eyes. I reached out, feeling for Adam's warm body. An empty expanse of cold sheet met my fingertips.

Was he downstairs already, making my tea? I turned my head, listened for sounds in the house: chatter drifting up from the kitchen, the sizzle of frying bacon. Maybe Sam on the landing, kicking forbidden goals into the open shower, or Molly, practising dance moves in her bedroom to Billie Eilish at top volume.

Nothing.

Just a thick hush. An air-conditioning unit hummed above. My ears rang.

Outside, the throttle of a bus as it pulled away. A thought dropped like a pebble in a distant pond. *Buses don't go past our house.*

Something wasn't right. I struggled to rise into consciousness. Thoughts rose and scattered. Was I at home? Had I gone back to the Airbnb with the girls? The more I tried to catch a thought, the more it darted away, like fish in shallow water.

My focus blurred as I forced my eyes open, lifted my head to look at Adam's pillow. It was tucked neatly under the duvet, no sign of the indentation of his head. Beyond, red digits winked 11.18. I didn't recognise the bedside table.

Where the hell was I?

I sat up and what felt like marbles rolling in my head made me cry out. My stomach clenched. Cold air hit my skin and I pulled the duvet over my breasts. Where was my T-shirt? Something caught at my neck and I touched the silver heart Adam gave me. I never wore this to bed. Never slept naked.

I glanced round the room. At the foot of the bed, a long desk, an office chair, a television above. Grey morning light cracked at the edges of full-length curtains beside the bed.

A hotel room.

My heart thudded. A trickle of sweat ran down my back.

'Emily?' I called.

Suddenly I was praying I was in the cosy Airbnb flat we'd dropped our stuff at yesterday evening and the girls were in the living room, Emily making coffee, Sunena and Lucy chatting on the sofa.

'Emily? Sunena?' My voice raw.

Images pierced my mind of the bar last night: flashing lights, thumping music. Banging hips with Sunena as we boogied; Lucy ordering an Orgasm cocktail, all of us singing, fist pumping to *I Will Survive*.

I rubbed my temples. But then I'd decided not to stay. I'd wanted to get an Uber home, so I'd be fresh to start on the launch strategy this morning. I'd got up to leave early. More images flashed: Lucy waving her glass, slopping blue gin down her sparkly top, shouting over the music's throb. 'Nina, don't be a party pooper. Don't go yet.' Sunena lunging across the table to hug me, crying, 'Bloody goody two-shoes, Neen. Screw boring old work.'

Collecting my coat, heading past the bar…. Then?

Nothing.

I shook my head as if I could rattle the memories loose.

'Emily?' My voice cracked.

The room's hush pressed back on me.

Why was I alone?

The room was grey, corporate. This wasn't an Airbnb. On the low bucket chair by the window my purple dress was folded neatly. Who folded that? Certainly not me. Adam was always chasing after me, picking up my stuff. Even my heels stood weirdly to attention, and were scuffed now, my sequin evening bag zipped shut and centred on the coffee table.

I shut my eyes. I couldn't remember getting undressed. I couldn't remember going to bed. I held my throbbing head in my hands. How much had I drunk? And I'd promised myself I wouldn't drink too much. I took a deep breath. This was insane. I was too old for nights like this.

I got out of bed and my knees buckled, as if my legs didn't belong to me. I reached out to steady myself on the mattress.

My stomach heaved.

I grabbed the dress, held it in front of me and stumbled to the window. I pulled back the curtain. Dark glass, stacked floors of desks and vacant office chairs glowered back, the sky a lid of grey. I spread a hand on the pane, peered into the narrow street below. The pavement was slick, an old newspaper gusting down double yellow lines. A car roared down the street, bass thumping, sluicing water into the gutter. I dropped my forehead to the cold glass. My skin pulled, sore above my eyebrow. I touched it and a small cut stung. Where had that come from?

Naked, shivering, I turned and fumbled in my bag for my phone. It was switched off. Odd. I jabbed and it flashed back to life. Immediately it rang, shattering the silence. I jumped, nearly dropped it.

'Nina? You got home alright then.'

My eyes filled at Emily's cheery voice. For a moment I couldn't speak.

'No.' I swallowed. 'I'm in a hotel room.'

'What?' A pause. 'Are you with someone?' Her voice a whisper, puzzled.

'No. Course not.'

'But…' A pause. 'Why'd you go to a hotel? Why didn't you come with us?'

My legs trembled and I dropped to the bed. The phone shook in my hand. My heartbeat pulsed so loud in my ears I could hardly hear.

I blinked to stop the tears falling. 'I don't know. I've no idea where I am. Or how I got here.'

Hearing the words out loud, I breathed in sharply. So did Emily as the same thought occurred to us both.

Someone brought me here.

All the breath seemed to have been squeezed out of my body. The hairs rose on the back of my neck.

Silence hung in the air. My mind reeled, scrabbled in the dark.

'Fuck, Nina.' Another pause.

Behind Emily, the chatter of Lucy and Sunena's voices, the babble of a television. 'Are you okay? Are you hurt?'

I clung to her voice like a lifeline. 'I feel terrible.'

'Are you safe?' Emily's voice, insistent now. 'You sure you're alone?'

I glanced over my shoulder towards the door, suddenly alert. Might someone be in the room with me? My heart thudded so hard it nearly burst out of my chest. I glanced round and my eyes flicked to the closed bathroom door. I tiptoed over, pressed my ear to it, straining in the silence, but my heartbeat pulsed so hard in my ears I couldn't hear anything. I raised my fingers, trembling. Nausea fizzed in my stomach. I pushed hard and the door flung back, thudded as it hit something behind.

The bathroom fan hummed. I stepped onto smooth tiles and checked behind the door. I leaned against the door jamb, my whole body shaking.

'No one's here.' I said into the phone.

An intake of breath on the end of the line. 'Just get out of there, Nina. Get out right now.'

Chapter Two

Emily stayed on speaker while I hurried to dress, her distant presence reassuring.

My stomach lurched as I noticed my pants and bra, folded in neat triangles on the chair. I never folded them like that.

So who the hell had?

My hands shook as I tried to pull the knickers over my feet, but I couldn't seem to control my legs and my toes caught in the fabric. It felt gross putting on last night's clothes. Leaning over made bile rise in my throat and I sat back on the bed, the phone beside me, gasping. My fingers trembled as I reached behind to fasten my bra but the clasp refused to catch. I swore.

Emily's voice, concerned. 'Nina. Nina. Are you alright?'

'Yeah. I feel really weird.' My voice broke. 'Dazed.'

'It's okay. Take your time, sweetie. I'm right here,'

Her voice continued, soothing as I stepped into the too tight purple dress.

'Do you remember getting to the hotel?'

I pulled the fabric up over my body and pushed my arms into the short sleeves.

'No.' I croaked. 'I don't remember anything.'

Emily released a long breath. 'Christ.'

I nodded as I tugged at the zip. 'The last thing I remember was the bar. Coming out of the ladies, putting on my coat...' My voice trailed away.

Emily's voice was false with cheery calm. 'It's okay sweetie. We'll work it out.'

Outside a police siren wailed and I startled.

I forced my feet into my pinching heels and grabbed my bag. As I turned to leave, I caught sight of myself in the mirror. My reflection stared back, hollow-eyed, white-faced, a ghostly parody of glamour above the low-cut dress and sequin bag. Mascara smudged on my cheeks, deepened the shadows under my eyes. I reflexively licked a finger and tried to wipe the make-up away. My lips were pale but swollen. I pressed them together and a small cut on my lip stung. I smoothed my unbrushed hair, fingering it like a comb, but lifting my arms made them ache.

On the counter, two brown key cards lay one on top of the other, Room 642, The Paddington Regent, WC4, embossed in gold on the front. My eyes widened at the address.

How the hell had I got *here*?

I snatched them up. 'Em, I've found key cards. I'm at the Paddington Regent.'

A sharp intake of breath. 'Paddington? Bloody hell. That's miles away.'

'I know.' My voice trailed away.

There was a pause. 'Okay Neen. Just go down to reception and wait for us there. You'll be nice and safe there...' She was using her gentle voice, the one she used with George and Scarlett when they'd fallen over and cut their knees.

I breathed in. 'Em. Please? Can you make an excuse to the others? Come on your own? I don't know what's... happened.' I breathed in. 'I, I don't want everyone to know....' My voice trailed off to a whisper.

'Of course.' Her voice understanding. 'Look, I'll jump in an Uber. I'll be with you in half an hour. Just go downstairs, now. You hear me, Nina? Go downstairs and wait for me.'

I nodded, tears pricking at my eyes. Then the phone went dead and Emily had gone. I hurried to the door, pulled it open and peered out, my heart thudding. A hushed corridor of worn patterned carpet stretched into the distance. I staggered, passing rows of doors shut like sentinels and followed the sign to the Lifts. A grey-haired woman in a dark coat was waiting and her eyes widened as she glanced at my dress and looked away. My cheeks burned, I'd seen the judgement in her glance and although I felt reassured by her presence, I tucked the sequin bag under my arm, out of sight. A lift arrived and we both stepped in, not looking at each other.

Something about the bright red hearts on a Valentine's dinner advert tugged in my mind. I felt dizzy and leaned back against the wall. My phone binged and I pulled it out. Adam.

Hope you had a fun evening
and a good night's sleep!
Let me know what train you're on xxx

My stomach clenched. Adam.

I shut my eyes. He'd have made the kids pancakes by now, and be chivvying Sam to clean his rugby boots, get his kit packed. I pictured them in the kitchen, Adam good naturedly beating the batter, Sam smearing Nutella over his pancake as if he was mortaring a brick, hot chocolate moustaching his upper lip, Molls scrolling through TikTok on her phone. My shoulders sagged. How I wished I was with them right now.

I started to reply, but my chest tightened.

Shit. *Adam.*

The lift pinged, the doors opened and I followed the woman out into the hotel lobby. It was bigger than I expected and the mixed smells of coffee, frying bacon and cleaning fluid made me queasy. From the breakfast room came the clink of cutlery on china, the metallic clang of lids from chafing dishes, the buzz of chatter. The hotel was all faded grandeur. A dusty glass chandelier dominated the lobby, hanging over a curved staircase with a chipped wrought-iron banister. A faux gilt-framed sign propped at the bottom welcomed a wedding party. Across the lobby, bay windows leaked weak daylight onto the cracked terracotta and cream marble floor tiles. At the reception desk, a turbaned man in a burgundy waistcoat served an older couple with wheelie bags by their feet.

I felt conspicuous in my dress and slunk over to the sofas below the windows and sat down. Behind me, a middle-aged man in a bright red puffa jacket was on the phone, another older couple, mackintoshes folded over the arms of the sofa, were having coffee, suitcases upright beside them. People scurried across the lobby, coming and going through the faded revolving doors behind me. I felt safe here.

The messages on my phone seemed to burn in my hand. Adam. Oh god. What could I tell him?

A text pinged from Molly.

Where's my purple leotard?

Swiftly followed by another from Sam.

Can't find my white shorts?

I replied to each

Hanging in the utility room, love you xxx,

In your drawer!!!! Look again xxx

I breathed in. I had to reply to Adam. I shut my eyes, remembering his cheerful face as we said goodbye yesterday. Me, babbling as I pressed a list of the kids' pick-up times into his hands, instructions about meals in the fridge and helping with French homework, whilst frantically trying to think what else I might have forgotten. His eyes smiling, the easy way he'd swung my bag into Emily's boot, then pulled me into a big hug. 'Text if you decide to come back tonight. Otherwise have a good time and we'll see you tomorrow.'

I felt sick.

I composed blandest message I could think of.

Really fun last night. Still having coffee. Love you so much xxx

My stomach clenched at the lie. But I needed time to think. What to tell him. How to tell him. The wounds were healed over now, but I knew they lay raw under the surface.

And what had happened? I shivered in the cold draughts from the revolving door and twisted the gold wedding band on my finger. I was a 43-year-old mum with two kids and a job. What was I doing here? Why couldn't I remember anything?

KATHRYN ENSALL

A Beautiful Girl

Synopsis

*A young woman goes in search of her sister who was trafficked for sex when they were children. **Jaz** was eleven when she witnessed her fourteen-year-old sister, **Lisa,** being lured into the sex trade within their Pennine town, and has been haunted by the experience ever since.*

*Eleven years on, Jaz is living a very different life in London, having won a place on a physics research programme. She is also involved in a tender love affair with an older transgender man, **Eddie**. Inwardly though, Jaz relives the details of Lisa's tempestuous life leading up to her disappearance. She recalls the brutal realities her sister faced, and the poverty that eventually overwhelmed her, and might have also crushed Jaz, if not for the intervention of a sympathetic teacher.*

Jaz decides to make her sister's experience public. Eddie, a journalist of some standing, helps organise a press event, where it's the other young trafficking survivors invited to speak that have the greatest impact. As Jaz is pulled into the lives of three of these survivors, she must deal with not only the pain of her own past, but also the discovery of a violent and inhumane world that enriches men at the expense of society's most vulnerable women. A world that survives unchallenged and often in plain sight.

Lisa's unknown fate hovers over the entire story. Past and present converge when Jaz and Eddie are drawn back to the Pennines. It's here that Jaz begins to dig beneath the surface of Lisa's life, unearthing layers of subterfuge and deceit. Yet despite all the secrecy, there's a hard clarity to what Jaz finally begins to understand. When you're enmeshed in a nightmare the challenge is to survive, but miraculously Lisa did more than that — she somehow found the courage to fight back.

ONE
THE BODY CON

Lisa was wearing a lime-green dress, her breasts swelling like little half-moons out of the neckline. It clung as tight as any dress could, and down each side there was a wide black stripe that started at her armpits and snaked around the edges of her tiny bust and into her waist and out around her hips down to the hem. It was a body con dress, as Lisa put it, meaning it was intended to make her look curvier than she really was.

I remember staring up at her, feeling completely baffled. Lisa's style was skinny jeans and sneakers, logo T shirts with a hoodie on top. Summer or winter, she wore exactly the same thing. She looked like an imposter in the dress, especially once you noticed her bare arms, which were pale and sharply angled and still had a child's thinness that made her look curvy in an upsetting way. It was this, I decided, her arms, that stopped the body con from working.

I was eleven at the time. Lisa had just turned fourteen, and was standing in the space between our two beds, gawking at herself in the bedroom mirror. I think of her now as being like a cygnet just out of the nest. Her great life adventure was starting and she knew no fear, stood there, wobbling on high heels, bathed in the sickly yellow light of our bedside lamp. 'Look at me,' she said proudly, sticking out her rib cage to make her breasts bloom bigger in the push-up bra. I *was* looking. It was hard not to. She was transformed, it was true, but no one would have taken her for a woman. I liked her a lot more when she looked like she usually looked, and didn't wear so much makeup, which – and I wasn't lying – was pasted on so thick it made her skin look synthetic and her eyes too large in proportion to her face. Maybe if she was going on stage, makeup like that would be useful. But just for going out in Littleton, I didn't see the need.

'Why're you done up like that?' I asked. Lisa glared at me with an expression that said, *fuck off nosy parker*, before pushing past me to reach for the white puffer jacket hung on the back of the door. This was also new, and had a fake fur trim. Very flash. How she could've afforded it I didn't know. She pulled the jacket over her bare bony shoulders, the silky lining crackling against her skin, and shoved her arms down into the sleeves. Straightaway her body looked put back together again. Not quite like that of a fourteen-year-old girl, but at least a little less weird.

She turned to take one last searching glance in the mirror. One last nervous breath. 'Right, I'm off,' she said.

So many questions pressed on my tongue I had to bite down on it to stop them coming out. One thing I'd quickly learned was that asking Lisa anything about her new job risked sending her through the roof. The week before, when she'd first told me about it, referring to the place she worked as *The Club* and excitedly flashing her fake ID, I'd been unable to hide my surprise. 'You're not old enough to have a job,' I said, only to feel the crack of her hand on my head, like a hundred fireworks bursting between my ears. What she didn't explain in that moment was that the whole thing was supposed to be a secret. I came to understand that later, when I went to sit on her bed, to cross-examine her, like I usually did, and she refused to tell me anything more about it. Which was pure torment for me. Lisa had always talked to me about what she was doing. Not that she'd ever had a job before. She'd mostly spent her evenings hanging out with the misfits in the Tesco carpark, ingesting all kinds of dubious substances and generally getting up to no good. Even through the freezing December nights, when icy winds numbed her nose and ears and pierced her thin hoodie. I used to worry she'd be picked up by the police, but now that she no longer frequented the Tesco carpark, all that began to seem quite harmless, compared to whatever secret thing she was up to at *The Club*.

To get there, she told me, she caught the number 24 bus from outside the Taj Takeaway, down to the ring-road turnoff at Tewdale Street. I knew the bus routes well, which was why the idea of Lisa getting off at Tewdale Street made me slightly nervous. Especially when she wouldn't tell me where she went after that. She had a short walk, she said, and grew even more vague when I asked where the club was.

'Near there.'

She let the words hang in the air, leaving me to finish her journey in my own mind. I pictured her, stepping down off the bus, onto a dark empty street, hood pulled over her face, thumbs all over her phone. She had a look about her, as Mum always said, of someone far too small for the big person she tried to be. But where was she going? The only place I could think of in walking distance of Tewdale Street, was the no-go area behind the old Odeon, and I couldn't imagine her going there on her own. The idea of that seemed absurd. Until I realised that what was absurd to me was unlikely to be absurd to Lisa. She went where she wanted, even when people told her she shouldn't. No one had ever been able to stop her. She fought till the very last if ever anyone tried.

'But where exactly?' I said, getting more uneasy by the minute.

'Oh, you won't be interested,' she said, which was the sort of thing she liked to say when it was obvious I was extremely interested.

That was how it began: the mystery of *The Club*. I'd watch her getting ready to go out, fascinated by her many grooming rituals, her hair straightening and leg shaving, her nail polish application. At first, if she was in the right mood, she'd offer to paint my toenails at the same time. On these occasions I'd get to sit on her bed, with my feet up on the bedside table, while she talked through the technique as solemnly as a maths teacher demonstrating long division. But I never concentrated on what she was saying because it was just nice sitting next to her and having her do something for me. She gave me other beauty tips, such as how to run a smear of Glitter and Glow down the front of my bare shins, so that my legs glistened as I walked. I laughed at this, but Lisa couldn't see what was so funny. I wondered then if perhaps she thought she wasn't beautiful enough to go out as she really was? If perhaps she thought she only stood a chance if she wore that type of dress and a lot of makeup? She was always saying she had terrible skin, when the truth was it wasn't terrible. But rather than let people see it, she'd cover it up with thick tan foundation. Personally, I didn't believe in all that stuff; makeup and nail polish. The only reason I showed an interest was to sit close to Lisa while she showed me how to put it on.

'Makeup makes me feel good,' she said. Though I saw no sign of it as I watched her each night, gravely patting it on and smoothing it in and then yanking on the dress and cramming her feet into the pointy high-heeled shoes – whereupon there'd be a blizzard of bedcovers as she searched for her purse, phone and keys, which she stuffed into the puffer jacket pockets while sprinting out of the room and down the stairs, her heels a muffled drumbeat on the carpet, growing fainter and fainter until the street door banged shut and the sound was indistinguishable from the noise of traffic on the road.

* * *

Home was a rented flat above the fish and chip shop on Oldham Road. Dad had moved out two years before, leaving just the three of us – Lisa, Mum and me – to get on with life by ourselves. We ended up with Mum, in part, because kids were expected to stay with their mothers, but mostly because Dad hadn't wanted us living with him. He wasn't a man with chil-drearing skills, he told us, and no one had reason to doubt it. From then on, until the day I left for university, the Oldham Road flat was my home. At first we missed Dad quite a lot, but Lisa and I never knew if Mum tried to arrange for us to visit him, because the subject didn't come up. And we never enquired if Dad had asked to see us, so as not to hear that he hadn't.

If we'd had somewhere else to go, some other family member to live with, we'd almost certainly have left. But the truth was we hadn't got anyone other than Mum. When she went down the pub and didn't come back for days – or when she did come back with her eyes a bleary red, and her speech slurred, and lay slumped in bed, leaving us with nothing to eat in the house – we prayed that she'd get arrested, or choke to death on her own vomit, so that we might go into foster care. We even considered other options, such as suffocating her while she slept, or putting ground-up rat poison in her food, but neither of us had the stomach for that, even though, of all the mothers in the world, ours had to be the worst.

In return for us not killing her Mum was barely grateful, and hardly ever pleasant. But she was someone I lived in fear of so I mostly did as I was told. Lisa did what she felt like. This was because she'd reached a stage in her development when she'd decided to take no notice of Mum. She said it was related to what happened when we were small, and she'd been handed the responsibility of keeping me alive, just so Mum and Dad could go down the pub. She'd had to feed me and wash me and more or less bring me up, which she managed remarkably well, considering her age. I remember how Mum and Dad's drinking crew used to praise her for it, as if Lisa had actually chosen the role for herself. They described it as 'useful experience' for later in life, as if there was nothing wrong with leaving a six-year-old in sole charge of her baby sister, just so they could spend the evening getting drunk.

All this had the drastic effect of making Lisa livid as hell, though she was mostly kind to me and had always been surprisingly patient when, as a three-year-old, I crawled all over her and sat on her chest and stroked her face with my sticky little hands. Or when I wandered out onto the pavement, strewn with garbage from the shop. If she had things to do, she used to put me in my cot and collect together my dolls and lay them on top of my filthy covers with their stubby plastic legs sticking out. If I started crying or looked beseechingly at her, she'd lift me out and sit me down where I could see what she was doing. That way she could get on with warming the milk for my cereal or rinsing the pots in the sink. I was too young then to feel bad about her having to do all that, and then later, when I did feel bad, I was unable to put it into words. I was also unable, for a long time, to draw the connection between Lisa's annoyance with our parents and the way we lived. Now I think that, if not for me, Lisa might have had a better childhood.

She was everything I was not. She was resilient and I was a whinger. She was fearless and I was a coward. At school, or out in the street, she fought anyone who challenged her. Great hulking girls and sometimes boys, scratching and spitting at them like a cat. Though she was little more than skin and bone. She said fighting was in her blood, and that she got it from Dad. But I didn't inherit any of that combative spirit. If a fight broke out, I ran away. At school Lisa was known as uncontrollable. She hated authority and had been suspended more times than anyone could remember. For a period, when she was nine or ten, she forcibly took food from the lunchboxes of other children and brought it home for us to share; fruit yogurts and Dairylea Triangles, things that Mum never bought. We enjoyed them too, until some teacher noticed. But the teachers didn't understand the conditions we lived in. It never occurred to them that Lisa was stealing because we were hungry. They thought she had behavioural problems. Neither did she try to explain to the small committee convened to punish her. It had to do with what she saw in their faces, she said, which was something rigid and unforgiving. They accused her of selling the food on to earn money to buy cigarettes, and Lisa never said a thing to defend herself. She shouldn't have been suspended that time, but she was. She took the punishment with her customary indifference, her face cold and hard from all the telling off.

If Mum had wanted, she could've gone in and explained. She could've helped Lisa get out of trouble. But Mum wasn't the kind to help. She was the kind who sucked all hope out of a situation and endlessly complained about not getting what she wanted. Not the kind who knew how to improve things, or set them right. She didn't even begin to try. I don't think Mum knew about the history of the world and all the people who'd succeeded against the odds. All the great scientists and reformers who'd changed things for the better, even though they'd come from nothing. The writers and artists who persisted for half their lives and overcame all kinds of setbacks until their voices were finally heard. What Mum knew was not to expect much. She said that girls like us would always have trouble making our way in the world, and that in the end, when life didn't turn out as we would've liked, no one could accuse her of not having warned us.

G.G. GANE

Thin Skin

Synopsis

Thin Skin *is a contemporary, speculative and psychological fiction, set in an alternate world where emotional trauma manifests as physical trauma on the body. Starting at birth, these wounds large or small – called Burdens – play an important and deeply personal part in everyday life. We follow an unnamed unreliable narrator into adulthood, secretly incapable of manifesting Burdens. Fearing exposure and becoming a pariah they fake their Burdens by self-harming, quickly learning to emotionally manipulate others for selfish gains. But how far will their extortions take them?*

Through the lens of this strange reality themes of mental health, prejudice, family and grief are explored in dark, sardonic fashion. The story is divided into three acts, each chronicling a snapshot of the narrator's life – childhood, adolescence, adulthood – and their growing sociopathy.

Act one sets the foundation for the narrator's lie, learning to fake Burdens to manipulate others. In doing so they perform research into the formation of Burdens by killing a young friend's cat and observing the effects it has on her. Act two tells the continuation of the lie as the narrator is tested by a school bully, RIO, trying to uncover the truth. Rio's pressure reveals how far the narrator will go to keep their secret as they lure her onto a deadly stretch of train track, killing her. Act three witnesses the conclusion of the lie as the narrator secures a job promotion through their manipulations. However, the true conclusion and catastrophe comes after the death of their turbulent little brother, DANIEL, forcing them into a life changing decision; in order to maintain the lie, they must fake a proportional Burden by cutting their own arm off...

THIN SKIN

At eight the nail of my left little toe died, creasing and curling, lifting like puff-pastry, until finally falling off. I watched, curiously, the pressurised tide of black blood rising within the pale pink digit, turning the outer corners a dirty tobacco-yellow. Wiggling the toe – foot suspended in mid-air – I flicked, wincing with delight at the pain, then, crowbarring a fingernail under, gently levered. The lid wouldn't come off its pot just yet.

'Not ready. Soon.'

I had decided to keep the news of my blackened toe a secret until the time was right, I had to maximize the surprise. Mum and Dad would flip, I was sure of it. After eight years of their worried eyes scanning my virgin flesh they'd finally have something to talk about. I could see them now, all smiles and laughter – weird. I had up until that point never understood people's hunger to fit in, like starving animals at the trough. I socked my foot and left the room. I was late for the funeral.

My family stood in the garden, cupped around a spade sized hole in the turf. Worms sliced through by the blade squeezed their guts out, down onto Mittens mummified in paper kitchen towel. Blue elephants squirting water were stamped on the bubbly paper.

'We're gathered here to remember Mittens,' said Dad, 'never was there a more loyal and honest rat as he.'

'Be at peace Mittens,' said Mum, holding the puffy Daniel and glancing sideways at me through a swollen black-eye. I wished she wouldn't; every so often she or Dad would stop what they were doing and scrutinise me, usually in moments of "heightened emotion" – whatever that meant – to check my reaction. Always to no avail, except for my irritation. This time though, something *was* happening. A balloon was expanding in me, crushing my lungs and tightening my chest. I hoped desperately it would burst. 'Something up, Poppet?' asked Mum.

'No. Nothing to see here. And don't call me that.'

But *something* was up and apparently visible.

'Your face, Poppet?'

I touched my face, it was wet. Strange. I rubbed my damp fingers together. Dad plonked the round of earth back into the ground with his good arm, eliminating Mittens from the world. He looked around, a glimmer in his eye.

'All okay, Hun?' he asked.

'Yes. Nothing to see here,' I said as I turned sharply on my heels and marched back to the house, 'And don't call me that!' I shouted back.

Later in bed, my bloomed toe sticking out from the rucked-up sheets. I thought about Mittens (Mum had wanted a cat), the only living thing I'd ever consider a friend. Small for his species – a runt – he could sit comfortably in the centre of a palm, staring from black beady eyes like the heads of twin pins with mottled grey-brown fur and a touch of black around his pink nose, pink too were his human-like hands with which he would cling to a finger whilst delivering that ghoulish gaze, also pink was his tail, bearing a kink half way up and sticking out at an odd angle from his body, the only other relief of colour against his dark frontage was the long knife-like teeth he flashed; he was, in short, a rat. I listed all the things he'd done that I'd liked. He once peed on Dad's lap. He once bit me. He once ate a whole Babybel that someone left out on the side. He once figured out how to use the cat flap (that Mum had planned on using for a cat) and climbed up onto the bird table in the garden and attacked the birds. He once ran across the dining table and stole food off Dad's plate. He once disappeared for three days, finally turning up covered in bright red paint. He once jumped into a full glass of white wine and stank of grapes for an entire week. He once snuck into the fridge and ate his way into the centre of a roast chicken. He once found his way into the pocket of Dad's dressing gown and pooed. He once bit Mum. He once made a nest in one of Dad's slippers. He once chewed through the cables of Mum's hair dryer, straighteners and Dad's electric razor. He once stowed away in Mum's handbag, where she later found him scurrying across her desk at work. He once ate six strong human pain killers and died.

'Maybe we should've only tried five.'

I thought back to the balloon. A strange thing crying. I'd never done it before. I didn't like it. I'd never do it again. Mittens, now in the world below, the world of worms and bottom feeders would never do *anything* again. I wondered how long it would take the worms to realise he was down there with them. It would be the paper with the elephants on that went first, surely, then the eyes.

Three days later the nail fell off. With one sock on and one sock off I strode into the front room holding it high in the air triumphantly. The room was full of adults (Mum and Dad's friends, who I'd met before but never bothered learning their names) sporting fat little black and blue babies bouncing on their laps. It was Daniel's first birthday. Everyone looked around.

'Oh, what have you got there, Pop?' asked Mum, holding out a slice of coffee and walnut cake I wasn't aware Daniel had developed a palate for. A man with a three fingered hand took the slice, gratefully.

'Toenail.'

'Toenail?' repeated Dad.

'Little toenail. Look,' gesturing with it toward the two of them. They rushed forward in disbelief. No-body touched their cake.

'Oh Poppet!' cried Mum, clapping her hands over her mouth and squinting through her black eye. At the corner of her puffed-up socket, set against its dark, tender looking purple, I spied a glimmer of a tear. What was it with wet faces that signify emotion?

Dad pointed to the scabby square left behind from the nail, 'From there? Ha! Amazing!' he shouted, reaching up with his good arm to the ceiling in joy.

The two doubled their hunching, studying the dried black flake pinched between thumb and forefinger, their faces grotesquely large in my vision. I winced from the proximity of the two pore covered lumps in front of me, taking half a step back. Silence hung in the room. I wasn't sure what would happen next. I'd mulled this moment over in my mind for years but had never been able to reach a satisfying conclusion. Finally, Daniel, a silver birthday cone strapped to his bruised head, burped and the tension broke. Everyone picked up their cake forks.

Dad straightened, letting out a hiss of relief, looking around the room quickly. Mum took me by the shoulders, looking around too. I didn't get it, the room was as unremarkable as before I'd entered: a rapidly disappearing cake, bruised babies, dull adults. One or two sets of eyes were still on me though.

'Come on,' said Mum, 'let's get you fixed up.' She called over my head, 'keep an eye on Dan, will you? We're just going to palliate Pop.'

'Okay,' someone said.

I was ushered into the kitchen. Once the three of us were alone Mum and Dad conferred furtively.

'I can't believe it's finally happened.'

'I know.'

'It's amazing.'

'This is amazing.'

'I can't believe it.'

'Nether can I.'

'What do we do now?'

'What normal parents do.'

'Palliate?'

'Palliate.'

'It's a miracle.'

'I can't fucking believe it.'

'Don't swear.'

'Wait, we have to be sure it's a genuine manifestation.'

'Right. Oh God I hope it is.'

Mum took me by the shoulders again. Dad crouched behind her. 'Pop,' she said, voice strained with supressed emotion, 'why did your toenail fall off?'

'Not sure,' I replied, alarmed at their reaction.

'Think, Pop!' she hissed.

'Hun,' said Dad, 'we need to know if it's conventional or a Burden. Can you tell us? Did anything fall on your toe to make the nail fall off?'

'No.'

'When did it start Pop?' asked Mum, 'When did it start to fall off?'

'When Mittens died.'

They turned to each other, hugging.

'It's a Burden, it's a Burden,' sobbed Dad.

'This is it,' whispered Mum, buried in his neck.

'This is what?' I asked.

Mum broke away from Dad, instead wrapping herself around me, sobbing. I froze. Her emotions whipped around me like a tree in a storm.

'This is what?' I asked again.

'No time for that now,' said Dad, glancing over his shoulder at the kitchen door. 'Let's get you palliated.'

They sat me down on the floor with a first aid kit.

'What's that?' I asked.

'It's an alcohol rub. For your toe.'

It stung.

'And what's that?'

'A plaster. You know what a plaster is.'

I looked at my toe encased in the plaster.

'We were so worried we'd never get to palliate you,' said Mum.

'Okay,' I said, lost in the weirdness. 'What happens now?'

'Now,' said Dad, 'we go out and *talk* about our feelings.'

'Okay,' I said again, still lost.

Back in the front room. The cake had been reduced to crumbs. Damn it. I knew this was going to get weird.

It got weirder. Dad ushered me over to the sofa, where a space had been made for me between the three fingered man and a woman with a scarred face. I perched, eyes darting left to right, counting my exits. Before I could make a move however Dad returned plonking something down into my lap. My eyes widened, it was a slice of lemon drizzle cake, fat and glistening – my favourite. A fork was handed to me. A silver cone fixed to my head. I stared at the cake. The cake stared back.

'Let's talk,' said Mum, 'about how you *feel*.'

'Yes Hun-bun, how *do* you feel?' asked Dad.

Their eyes were hungry. I took a stab at an answer.

'Sad?' I said, spitting crumbs across the room.

'By the time I was your age I had already lost two,' said the three fingered man, smiling as he held up his gappy hand. 'I was bullied at school. One day he caught me on the way back from the pool and made me change back into my trunks, then stole all my clothes and forced me to walk home barefoot and nearly naked across town. Kids are cruel but my brother took it to another level. There were no barriers to his unkindness. He left me feeling alone, he more than just picked on me. It had a huge psychological effect. He's got a wife and children now, apparently. I think he acted up because our father was a drunk and left our mother when we were young.'

I blinked in response.

'When I was in my twenties, my fiancé at the time – Jack – cheated on me and left me for someone else,' said the woman with the scarred face, looking at her lap. 'I walked in on them. We were going to get married. We'd already sent out the invitations.' She touched her face just below her scar. A twisted kind of flame that rippled up from chin to brow on her left side, sweeping across an eye in the process, leaving it permanently half closed.

I blinked again.

Someone piped up from the other side of the room, 'my best friend had a stroke the other year – left me deaf in my right ear.'

And another voice, 'the girl that got away has just had a baby that should've been mine.'

And another, 'my dog was hit by a car, he'd been my friend for ten years.'

Another, 'I failed to get into the university I wanted.'

There was no stopping it, voices piled into one-another as the peal of crashing bells continued to ring around the room.

'My dentist told me I had gum disease.'

'I fear failure with everything I do.'

'I'm not as honest as I know I could be.'

'I regularly don't have enough money in the bank.'

'I had to have a mastectomy at twenty-six.'

'I can't sleep and don't know why.'

'My wife left me.'

'I cry when I wake up every morning.'

'I hate looking at myself in the mirror.'

'I didn't get the grades I wanted at school.'

'I don't know how to connect with my children.'

'I was circumcised at birth and haven't been able to come to terms with it.'

'I've just been fired.'

'My sister died, as you know,' said Dad, softly.

I looked at his withered arm, its little hand curled into a bony fist forever. Its skin waxy and yellow.

I put my folk down and looked at each person in turn, picturing their misshapen sorrows. After the chorus of confessions there was a stillness, all eyes focused on me – my turn, no more cake to chew. I hated eye contact, all that *emotion* that apparently goes with the brief connection of two sets of wet, rotating orbs. Gross. But there was something in the eyes that looked at me now, something I'd not see before. There was an interest there, a desire to take note that hooked me – against my better judgment – like a fish. Even the bruised babies were paying attention. This was my first foray into the world of *sharing*.

'Mittens…was…my favourite.'

I scratched my arm.

'He…liked to bite things.'

I looked at the ceiling.

'He…was small.'

I looked at the floor.

'He…lived in the corner of my room and I'd feed him and clean his cage and change the water and take him out for adventures and he had a funny tail, which I liked because it reminded me of me because I'm funny too, inside, and I sometimes put him down my top and he'd crawl all over me under my clothes scratching which tickled and I'd whisper to him all the weird things people did around me, like look at me funny or try to talk to me and I'd say "good night" to him every night and sometimes he'd squeak and sometimes he'd get into his wheel and run and sometimes he'd hide inside toilet rolls I'd give him.'

I paused for breath.

'And then when he died, I felt like something had gone inside me too and I felt empty and lonely and I miss him, I guess. And then there was a big balloon inside me. And then I *cried*. And then my toenail fell off.'

Everyone smiled. Daniel giggled. I squirmed.

'How do you feel, talking about it?' asked Dad.

'I don't know,' I said, knowing exactly.

'Because it's important that you feel free to talk about your emotions, Poppet. Like we all do,' said Mum.

'I know,' I said, not really knowing.

ROGER GRANT

Gray Matter

Synopsis

A rising star of neuroscience upsets world order when she discovers how a cure for dementia could change the meaning of life. Abi Bergkamp's research theories are far too radical for commercial neuroscience so she's learned to keep those to herself, but her landmark contributions to the field of brain-mapping has made her the Head of Research at NeuroGen. The biotech is making steady progress on its memory aid technology when one of Abi's new clinical trials subjects, Robert Okonjo, begins advancing rapidly ahead of the others.

Robert and Abi's lives are soon swept up together when their remarkable achievements trigger a frenzy of commercial interest and even celebrity. While helping each other endure the intensifying public attention, scientist and 'lab rat' break the golden rule and fall in love. Robert becomes gravely ill from the concentrated brain mapping. With only months to live he's offered the chance of an alternative existence, a life he can't bear to contemplate except that it comes from Abi, the woman he also can't bear to lose. Her research into artificial-consciousness is so controversial that the pair must work in secret. Abi finally discovers the pathway into the human mind that she has always searched. Soon afterwards, Robert disappears.

The public is horrified to learn of Robert's freakish existence; he's seized from Abi by the authorities and hidden away. In return for revealing her breakthrough science, Abi forces the Government to first grant Robert a public hearing over his right to existence and freedom. It sets society ablaze with debate over human rights, laws of nature and even the environment. Robert loses, but Abi has masterminded a complex deception for everyone and had no intention of sacrificing her soul mate to a government lab, nor revealing her contentious science to the world.

Author's Note
On its anticipated completion within 10-20 years the 'human brain map' is widely expected to spare the millennial generation, and possibly some of their parents, from ever having to suffer from dementia. But this will only be the beginning. Without drugs, surgery or therapy, the human brain map will also be used to treat epilepsy, Parkinson's, schizophrenia, autism, depression, OCD, phobias, addiction and almost every form of neurosis. The beginning will bring wondrous cures, but it may enable one cure, that for many, will go too far.

Neuroscientists in the field may consider the mapping of the entire human brain within 10 years ambitious. But how ambitious? In 1990 the Bush administration announced the commencement of a $3 billion project to map the entire Human Genome within 15 years. A working draft of the Genome was published in February 2000, five years ahead of schedule. Whether completing the human brain map takes an extra 10, 15 or 25 years beyond this story's time-line, it will still occur within the lifetime of someone alive today.

Every dollar we invested to map the Human Genome returned $140 to our economy — every dollar. Today our scientists are mapping the human brain to unlock the answers to Alzheimer's...Now is the time to reach a level of research and development not seen since the height of the Space Race.

President Barack Obama
State of the Union Address – 12 February, 2013

I wish I could tell you what a mind without limitation is really like. It's not what most people would imagine, but most people wouldn't imagine such a thing at all. Yes there are many moments of wonder, even awe, sometimes it's a heck of a power trip too, but, in between all that, it's largely about ordinary decisions, frustrations, long stretches of boredom, loneliness, just normal life really. I wish I could tell you why I allowed her to do this to me, or why more than half the world want me gone and the rest would probably follow in my path, if they could. But I still can't explain these things to myself and the effort often drags me down into one of my 'spells'. When that happens no relief will come through the normal passage of time, nor even from sleep.

I eventually stumbled upon a solution. I have to relive my ordeal in my mind step by step from the beginning. I start by remembering the very first event that kicked it all off to understand how I'd arrived at that first decision that led me to the next decision, and to the next, and so on until I arrive back at the present. Through this process I would relearn that each of my decisions was justifiable given what I knew at the time. Afterwards, I find peace, at least for a while. 'Connecting the dots' is the short hand expression I use to label this process. It takes a little while, but not as long as you'd imagine because I can think a lot faster now. The best part of having an eidetic memory is that you don't forget anything. And that's also the worst part.

When I connect the dots I need to sink into a type of meditative state and it's best to do so somewhere peaceful like the ridge of these low slung mountains where I can gaze out over the empty, timeless desert. Once again, the memories come flooding back from that dreary workday afternoon, when the package arrived.

New York City – 2030

'Delivery from…Neuro…gen? Shall I bring it over?' It was Caroline at the front desk.

'Nah, I'll be right out' I replied instinctively. Most people would have accepted the personal delivery but I was always looking for an excuse to get away from the suite. A trip to the front would give me a chance to steal a cookie from the barista station we'd installed for the clients. My heart sank as I spotted Spence in his familiar position leering over Caroline's desk and having a one way conversation with her. Caroline was our newest assistant editor, fresh out of college with a media studies degree. This post-house always put the new kid at the reception desk with an editing console and gave them the jobs no one else wanted like archiving rushes all day. If that wasn't bad enough they also had to double as a receptionist to save hiring an extra body. This would be a fate worse than death for most editors, but when you're 22 and get to watch all the happenings that never make it to the final cut of a popular TV show, you're the queen of your social group.

Caroline looked relieved when she saw me. Spence was already shaking my delivery box and reading the label like a kid on Christmas morning. 'Massachusetts Institute of Technology! What the hell are they sending *you*?'

'I dunno' was all I could think to mumble, suddenly very sorry I hadn't accepted the delivery. We were sworn to secrecy on the nature of our participation, nothing good would come from people knowing that you were recording their every move and word.

'So open it up, Bobbo, let's see. Maybe they're giving you an honorary PhD for services to the entertainment industry!' Few things annoyed me more than Spence calling me 'Bobbo', but one of those things was enduring Caroline having to laugh at her boss's unfunny joke at my expense. Another was that I also had to smile because Spence was my boss too, sort of.

'Oh I think it's just…my new glasses,' I said, surprising myself with a moment's inspiration.

'From MIT?'

'Uh no, it's an online optician based up near the campus there in Boston uh…borrowed the name I guess.' That sentence faded until barely audible at the end. I was stumbling into my first of many lies.

'Well let me and Caroline see them!'

'Uh, in a minute, I'll be right back. I need to start a render' I said. Starting a render is an editor's 'get out of jail free' card. Rendering is effectively making the computer start processing and saving all your changes in the editing software. Everyone knew how constant and time consuming renders were, and you couldn't continue working on a file while it was rendering for 5 minutes or even more. To maximise efficiency all bathroom, coffee and even lunch breaks were encouraged during 'a render'. Spence looked sceptical, but I didn't wait for an answer and bolted for my suite cradling my precious package in both arms like a running back with the ball. I had no intention of returning.

Back in the dimly lit safety of edit Suite Four I enjoyed a moment of smugness over this special project that I had to conceal from the *ordinary* people. I felt a bit like James Bond receiving his latest gadgets from Q. As I ripped open the box I was more anxious about how the glasses would look on me than I was about making medical history. Inside I found a good quality hard shell, black plastic case, presumably the one to use for packing the precious items in aircraft hold luggage. On its front were four manual combination lock tumblers next to a barely noticeable, postage-stamp sized black square, which I knew was the thumbprint scanner. To activate the scanner I set the lock tumblers to 1-9-9-4, my year of birth pre-arranged code, then pressed my thumb to it. The solid lid released with a reassuringly deep click to reveal the eyeglasses, baseball cap, and on-body data transmitter all sealed in clear plastic and snug in their black foam mouldings. In terms of the packaging, it looked more like I'd bought some trendy and expensive electronics rather than a pair of eyeglasses from the opticians. I was glad I hadn't opened the box at the front desk.

I'd chosen the black-rimmed nerd glasses like the ones Dr Bergkamp had passed around at the induction. I slipped them on and inspected them on my phone's screen. They were heavier than normal just as I was expecting, but I was taken aback by how much they dominated my face compared to my existing glasses that weren't dissimilar. I guess new glasses, like new haircuts, are always a bit of a shock at first. A quick look around the room confirmed the prescription was right. I shouldn't have been surprised by that, if NeuroGen could read my mind they ought to be able to fill an eyeglass prescription.

I unwrapped the baseball cap next. It was also heavy but I was pleased that its hidden sensors could not be felt through the padded fabric. I'd chosen a black cap with a white Japanese symbol on the front. I'd found the symbol in the online catalogue NeuroGen had directed us to, but I didn't know what it stood for. Overall, the gear seemed just about cool enough to wear. There was no revealing paperwork or instructions included in the box in case the parcel had gone missing. As instructed at the induction I immediately put the baseball cap on, unwrapped the on-body processor, snapped it onto my belt and dropped my t-shirt over the top. That was it. No wires, no power buttons, no nothin'; they didn't want the lab rats fiddling. The technology was body heat activated and NeuroGen controlled everything. I was on the clock and more than that, I was on the payroll! Would big brother call me to confirm that I'm on their radar? I figured I should just carry on as normal, so that's exactly what I did.

For once I was happy for the distraction of my latest Priya-Marie reality show assignment. I didn't want to go out and present my new cap and glasses to the mocking crowds, and they would be mocking. Few professions hone snide and cynical comment making skills like video editing. Bitter humour is our poultice for the sores caused by long days of trying to make lovable 'digital stars' appear real, and real 'human stars' appear lovable. In both cases we often have to make bad actors appear good actors and also fix the technical and creative foibles of everyone on the other side of the camera. The world sees the one great scene but we see a dozen botched ones and have to weave bits of each of them together to make the one *great scene*.

We are the forgotten ones, the rarely noticed, the untouchables of our industry. The ambiance of an edit suite near the end of a 16-hour session to deadline is not for the faint hearted. A constipated editor who sits in a stuffy room with no daylight. His nose filled with the smell of stale tuna sandwiches the clients wouldn't eat and the staff were forbidden to touch; his mouth tasting the bitterness of half a dozen coffees and his stomach churning with the emptiness that only comes from munching sugary biscuits all day. All this brews in the editor a perfect storm of acidic, barbarous, razor sharp wisecracks about the defenceless performers on his screen whose careers have been entrusted to his care.

'Let's see them then!' Spence had infiltrated my space and he'd dragged Caroline along for the ride.

'Yes, model them for us,' she giggled.

I was beginning to feel less sympathetic to her sufferance under Spence. There was nothing to do but dramatically spin around on my swivel chair to face them. I saw Spence's eyes widen and the cutting remark he'd been brewing seemed to stick in his throat. Had his instinct for ridicule been dampened by a genuine moment of pity?

'Oh my God, Bobbo,' he improvised, '...you really are the nerdiest guy in here! Did they send that hat with the glasses?'

'Yeah!' I agreed heartily, grateful for his explanation of the sudden appearance of the cap which I'd already forgotten was on my head. 'I like it,' I declared defiantly 'it's a keeper.'

'I like it too...and the glasses,' volunteered Caroline, not convincingly, but her charity instantly won her back into my favour. Spence had been holding the door wide open, no doubt with a plan to invite half the office in to share his unborn joke, but now, a fleeting moment of humanity had taken the wind out of this sails. He paused awkwardly to consider his exit strategy and as he backed out all he could think to say was 'oh well, at least no one will see you in here.'

'You're so *mean*!' I heard Caroline say just as the door clicked shut.

Given this most disastrous unveiling of my 'new look,' I worried that it may now seem odd for me to continue to wear this ensemble. Then again, the mob might just think that I march to my own beat – the true creative I am! I'd have to hope for that. I was dying to tell them I made $750 a week for wearing this cap and glasses, but I had to keep that to myself.

TAMARA HENRIQUES

Portrait of a Family

Synopsis

Portrait of a Family, *upmarket fiction set in the 1970s, tells the story of a family whose everyday life is torn apart when amateur artist MARGOT wins a prestigious art award, abandons her husband and uproots her nine-year-old twin daughters to kick-start her career.*

MARGOT (29) is married to IVOR (50), a painter. Ivor's dealer secretly enters Margot's work for the Bamcroft Award which includes a studio residency on the Bamcroft estate. When Margot wins, Ivor is consumed with jealousy and refuses to look after their daughters, NINA and CHLOE. As Margot has to finish seven paintings for the Bamcroft exhibition, six weeks away, she accepts the residency, taking the twins with her.

Obliged to attend a meeting with the Bamcrofts, she leaves her daughters alone in their isolated temporary home. The girls accidentally burn the studio down. Margot returns to find her children unscathed, but her paintings destroyed.

She tries to withdraw from the show until she learns that she is liable for costs and that her fledgling career will be over. Margot decides to paint at home in London until she discovers that BARBARA (25) has moved in with Ivor. Unwilling to admit failure, or go into debt, Margot flees to her own childhood home. Desperate to be with their father, Nina and Chloe run away to London.

Ivor welcomes the children but denies Margot access. Distraught, Margot paints furiously. Barbara tires of surrogate motherhood and suggests they keep her favourite child, Chloe, and return Nina to Margot. Appalled, Ivor realises that Margot, despite her faults, is a loving mother. Their summer of discontent is over but the children no longer trust their parents, only their sibling bond remains intact. One decade later, Chloe is a devoted mother and Nina is an artist. Margot achieves posthumous success.

Portrait of a Family
Chapter 1

The day my sister and I burnt the house down, our mother Margot was out with her dealer, Cosmo. Art not drugs. Margot's only vice was nicotine. And neglect, I suppose, but it was the 1970s, and she was an artist.

Apparently, she had an appointment to sell her soul. She ignored us when we asked whether it would hurt, staring out of the kitchen window with her back to us, while we ladled extra sugar onto our cornflakes.

We could tell she had been painting the night before because the fingers clasped around her mug of coffee were flecked with fresh blue paint; *turquoise blue* she would say. Margot painted at night, even after she had painted all day. The night before it had been a sky blue, that's *azure blue* by the way. She said she had to paint to heal her soul. It seemed a pity to sell it after all the effort of mixing all those special blues, but we didn't say anything. We were only nine.

Our mother didn't know that we had jimmied the bedroom window open with a screwdriver from the shed and put up a ladder so that we could climb out at night. We spied on her in her studio from the damp grass on the lawn, flitting towards her like moths in our nylon nighties, electrified hair flying around our faces. She held a cigarette in one hand and a paintbrush in the other, not seeing us - even when we pressed our noses flat onto the cold glass. Our mother was in a trance, and we had become invisible.

After breakfast that morning she said she had to change her clothes and we ran after her to watch, jostling each other up the stairs. We sat on the floor toasting our feet on the dodgy four-bar heater. Margot unzipped her painting overalls, *indigo blue* to you and me, and put on her dress; the mermaid green one that she wore on special occasions. We were wearing matching stripy t-shirts and navy terry shorts. Margot always dressed us in matching clothes. *In case I lose one of you*, said our mother, *then I can tell the police to look for a girl who looks exactly the same.*

It was jungle warm in the Bothy bedroom by the time Margot was ready. We wanted to stay in the muggy warmth with the heater ticking like a grandfather clock to keep us company, but she wanted us to wave goodbye.

'Remember girls: no swimming in the lake, and no playing dead on the road,' she said, tugging at the sticky door of her Datsun Cherry. It wasn't the colour of a cherry, it was Wotsit orange. We had driven from London in that car for hours and had avoided it ever since. Chloe had been sick on the backseat and the smell lingered.

'You forgot no darts,' I said, trying to delay her for a moment longer.

'Don't be cheeky, Nina,' said our mother, shoving her pictures into the back seat.

'We're not playing them again, ever, I'm scarred for life,' said Chloe, craning her chin over her shoulder, searching for the teeny tiny mark.

'I won't be long, girls, and I'll bring you both a bag of Pic'n'Mix,' said Margot, rushing back to kiss us on both cheeks and then our foreheads for luck.

Our mother must have been in a hurry to leave because she forgot to tell us to be good. The stone step was getting clammy under our bare feet while we watched her car bumping down the track. Once she had disappeared, we raced each other to the stables around the back. We weren't sure how long it took to sell a soul and we had to finish our bucket of poison.

It was for pouring onto intruders, like the encyclopaedia salesman who had sold us an engraved leather set that would *last us a lifetime*. After we showed Margot our new set of books, she told *us to never, ever, answer the door to anybody. There are criminals out there.*

'Is it deadly yet?' asked Chloe, squatting down with the plastic bucket wedged between her knees.

I stirred the poison with the yellow spade. We had thought we were going on a seaside holiday when we left home in the middle of the night. Margot had been whispering to us to *hurry, hurry, hurry* as we packed our bags with swimsuits and sundresses.

The Bothy wasn't anywhere near the sea. It was perched half way up a steep hill, surrounded by fields criss-crossed by tumbling stone walls and barbed wire fences that caught sheep fluff and dangled dead birds. Our optimistic sundresses hung in the cupboard, rattling on wire hangers, lonely like us. We gave up asking when we were going to the seaside and abandoned the bucket and spade. Until we found the weed killer in the shed and came up with the poison idea.

Our mother claimed to love living at the Bothy – or at least that's what she told Cosmo when he came to inspect her latest paintings. They were taller than us and neatly stacked up on the side of the studio walls. Cosmo told her that *she had to meet her collector and that no, she couldn't just hide us in the car*. We needed the bucket of poison to protect us from the criminals out there.

'It smells horrible but those swirly bits are like rainbows,' said Chloe, her hair grazing the oily surface.

'That's the petrol.'

We had found it in a rusty jerry can in the boathouse where we used to play before we got banned for paddling in the swampy lake. 'Let's add the weed killer.' I tore off the corner of the box with the skull and cross bones and sprinkled it onto the shiny surface. The powder formed a grey scum.

'It's gone all ugly,' said Chloe, hooking her hair away.

We both studied the mucky brew.

'It's definitely deadly now. It will kill in seconds,' I said.

We shunted the ladder over from the bedroom window so that we could rig up a trap with a rope tied onto the bucket. Chloe held the ladder steady while I climbed, the bucket sloshing at each step.

'It splashed onto my foot,' yelled Chloe.

The ladder started to twang, like a loose guitar string.

'It's getting all wobbly,' I shouted down.

'I can't stay down here, I'm going to get poison in my eye and then I'll go blind,' cried Chloe. 'I'm already scarred for life.'

'Please, Chloe, don't let go –' I leant backwards to check but she had already stepped away, wiping her foot in the grass. My foot slipped and I dropped the bucket. It tumbled and bounced its way down, spewing its contents, the rope like a tail behind it.

'Now look what you've done,' shrieked Chloe. 'I'm poisoned now, I'm going to die. Seconds from now.' She was hopping around on one foot.

I slithered down the ladder, its rungs thwacking at my bare legs, burning my knees. 'Thanks a lot, Chloe, thanks a lot for letting go, I could have fallen off and died,' I said, as I squelched into the mud.

'No. That's not fair,' shouted Chloe, close to my face, tiny bits of spit flying at me. 'You're the one who should say sorry to me. For killing me with all that poison you poured on me.' She was wiping her face with the back of her arm. 'You'll be sorry when I'm dead.'

We stood on the lawn snivelling; Chloe rubbing her arm and me rubbing my knees.

'I'm sorry, Chloe, I didn't mean to pour the poison onto you,' I said, chewing at my lip. 'How will we know when you start to die?'

'I'll turn black from the poison, obviously,' said Chloe. 'But I might not die. I kept my mouth closed.'

We both sighed like deflating balloons and then trudged indoors, trailing mud and disappointment. We plonked ourselves down in the living room, sulking in the gloom while the TV warmed up. We weren't meant to watch TV in the daytime, and we couldn't turn the light on because it fused the sockets.

The smell in the living room seemed worse than usual. I wiped my oily hand on the arm of the sofa and then sniffed with my nose in the air, pretending to be a cartoon dog. 'Can you smell smoke?'

'No, I can't,' said Chloe. She was sprawled on the smelly rug, plaiting the fringe, 'I can only smell patuli,'

'It's patchouli. Pat-choo-li.'

'Don't care. Still can't smell any smoke,' said Chloe, refusing to look at me doing my dog impression.

'Maybe there's a burning cigarette somewhere. Maybe there's an old one stuck under the sofa?' I said.

Chloe swivelled around like a clock dial and peered under the sofa.

'I think there might be an old chocolate at the back.' She tried to squish herself underneath.

'I hate it here and I wish we could go home,' I said. Chloe didn't answer so I jabbed her with my foot.

She reversed from the sofa and pulled out a hairy Rolo. 'Mummy says we can go home when she has finished her pictures,' said Chloe, wiping the chocolate on her shorts.

There was a thump directly above us, like an intruder with a wooden leg.

'Maybe there is actually a criminal,' I whispered. We crept over to the window and opened the curtains a crack but the driveway was empty. 'I wish I hadn't spilt the poison.'

Chloe nibbled around the Rolo.

'If I gave you 2p would you open the door and have a look?' I said to Chloe.

'How come you've got 2p?' asked Chloe, between chews.

'I found it.'

'Where d'you find it?' asked Chloe.

'Please, Chloe, just go and take a look.' The words rushed out.

'Alright, then.'

She trudged to the door. 'The doorknob's hot,' she said, flapping her hand.

'I'm not giving you my 2p until you open the door and take a proper look.'

Chloe stretched her stripy shirt over the doorknob and twisted it open. 'I can smell smoke now,' she said.

'Told you so,' I said.

'It looks like there's a grey cloud inside the house,' said Chloe.

I went over and stood close to her. We watched the smoke rolling down the staircase. When it reached the last step, I slammed the door and we scuttled back to our places; Chloe on the rug, me on the sofa. 'What do we do now?' said Chloe, kneading the rug.

'Let's just pretend we didn't see anything. Maybe it will go away.'

We pretended to watch TV even though it was the news.

'If there really is a fire, do you think we should try and put it out?' I said.

'I think this fire might be too big for us,' said Chloe. She moved from her spot on the rug and sat next to me on the sofa.

'Shall we ring 999?' I asked.

'Dunno,' said Chloe. 'I'd rather stay in here.'

The newsreaders were talking about Mohammad Ali dancing like butterfly and stinging like a bee but we weren't really listening and when we heard a roar that sounded like a dragon, we leapt up, wrenched open the door and ran blindly down the corridor and into the kitchen, slamming the door behind us. Our budgerigar was skittering in his cage.

'You dial the number and I'll do the talking.' I said.

I held the phone between both of our ears while Chloe slotted her finger into the number nine hole and pulled it around. We watched the dial whirr back into place. Three times.

The phone rang once.

'Emergency Services, which service do you require?'

I swivelled the phone onto my shoulder. 'What service do we require?' I asked Chloe. I hadn't expected a choice.

'Dunno. Just say there is a fire,' said Chloe. She was tugging at her tangled hair, prising it apart with her fingers as if it was very important.

'Our house is on fire.' The phone was slippery and smoke was sneaking under the kitchen door.

'Can I confirm that you are reporting a fire?' said the voice. She already sounded cross with us.

'Yes, it was upstairs. But now it's downstairs.'

'What's your address?'

We looked at each other, crooking our chins over the phone.

'It's a crime to waste police time and we will trace this call.'

'It's The Bothy. We don't know the address – we don't really live here. It's first left after the garage.'

'First right,' said Chloe, nudging me with her foot.

'Listen you two, we don't take kindly to pranksters calling this line. There might be a real emergency, someone might be having a heart attack and be in genuine need of our services.'

We turned away from the door and watched a waterfall of flames cascading down the kitchen window.

'It's ever so close to us now. It's huffing and puffing outside the door and it's raining flames outside,' I whispered into the phone, as if the fire could hear us.

'Well, if you could just give us your address we could –'

The phone line went dead and the kitchen door creaked open, slowly at first, then a wave of hot air barrelled into the kitchen. We dropped the phone, leaving it to dangle on its curly wire and burst out of the house, running with our heads down, hands on our ears to block out the angry bellowing, zig-zagging around the shards of glass smashing onto the cobbles.

We ran through the gate and past the stables, sobbing between jagged breaths. Thorny branches whipped our windmilling arms as we ran down the path towards the lake. We ran on and on, stitches stabbing at our sides until we got to the boathouse. We trampled through the nettles to get to the door and dropped down into the corner, hiding underneath the shelves at the back. Our chests were heaving.

'We are going to be. In such. Big trouble,' said Chloe, panting.

'Worst ever,' I said, clutching my ribs. 'Mummy's going to know we were watching telly in the daytime. We'll have to hide here for ages.'

We scrabbled backwards between the faded orange lifejackets. The boathouse floor was spongy and smelt of mouldy leaves.

'We left Houdini behind,' said Chloe.

'He's Houdini, he'll have escaped,' I said. 'But Mummy's pictures were inside.'

'We are going to have to drown ourselves in the lake,' said Chloe. 'Then nobody will be cross with us.'

We buried our cheeks between our knees and our pants were clammy from where we had peed in panic. We would have sold our own souls, whatever that entailed, to turn back time. Half an hour would have been enough.

FERGAL THOMAS McHUGH

Polar Terminus

Synopsis

Polar Terminus *is a literary novel about marriage, family, achievement, and happiness, set in a contemporary world that appears to be coming apart at the seams. It is also a book about time, identity, gender, and what it means to be human in an age of science.*

Denise Putnam and Jerome Abbott are a couple in their thirties, living in a remote farmhouse in New England. They are still recovering from the loss of an infant and deep cracks are emerging in their relationship. Jerome, magazine freelancer and newly minted author of a high-brow self-help book, has struggled in the shadow of Denise, a star academic, the first female, and youngest ever, full Professor of Philosophy at a prestigious north-eastern college. For the first time in recent memory, Jerome is getting attention too—but he has started to wander, not least in the direction of Cassie, Denise's globe-trotting violinist sister.

It is not just their marriage falling apart, there is something wrong, more fundamentally, with the world. Strange weather, planes vanishing from the sky, and a sense of impending disaster. All three have a complex relationship with an enigmatic opera-loving technology-titan, Alain Pelegrin, whose latest pet project, code-name 'Polar Terminus' might turn out to be a little more controversial—and a great deal more dangerous—than securing prominent donor plaques on the walls of national opera houses.

When Pelegrin disappears in disgrace, leaving investors clamoring, amidst talk of fraud on a history-beating scale, Jerome wonders how it will impact the people who orbited his star. Soon after, Denise disappears. Jerome goes in pursuit, looking for answers. Something is attracting him to the frozen north. There are answers there, for all of them. Just not necessarily the ones they are expecting.

Part 1: How to Go On

1. That Christmas Denise taught me how to play solitaire. She sat in the great room, cross-legged on the rug in front of the fire, and dealt the cards out in neat rows. It was early evening and already dark. I had slept through the afternoon, once again. If it had not been for the phone ringing in the hallway I probably would have continued to sleep.

'I am having difficulty believing that you never learned how to play this game.'

Denise was looking up at me. Waiting for a response. There was something indecipherable in her mouth and eyes, amusement perhaps, though it might have been disappointment or sadness. I shrugged, not committing either way. Denise continued to look up at me, for perhaps another second, though it seemed longer, before going back to dealing the cards.

'Actually, I can believe it,' she said in a careful, considered way as if coming to the end of a knotty chain of reasoning.

'Teach me then,' I replied.

I sat down beside her on the rug.

'There are a hundred and more variations of solitaire but the version I'm going to teach you now, Klondike, is the best known. This is a game of exile, of displacement. Think of those gold-prospectors in their camps at night, up in the frozen north. The game can also be played with a Tarot deck, though here, as you can see, I am using the standard 52-card, French-suited deck.'

A small pocket of gas trapped inside one of the logs burning in the hearth ignited with a groan and then a loud popping sound. A dense cloud of tiny golden sparks rushed up the chimney accompanied by a noisy gulp of air. I startled. I probably should have been reminded of the forest fires which had ravaged the hills overlooking Haven through most of December, dominating the news cycle, even here on the east coast. But instead, I was thinking about the sound of glaciers calving. It wasn't only ice crystals breaking down; time itself was coming loose up there, and the receding ice was revealing secrets and artifacts from a past so distant it might as well have been our future.

'I call it patience,' I said.

'What?' Denise said, as if I had responded to something she had thought but not verbalized.

'Solitaire. The game you are playing. I call it patience.'

Denise sighed.

'Of course you do.'

2. Christmas had been cold but without any fresh snow. And then, as the New Year approached, our remote corner of New England was pounded by a storm coming down from the northeast, unloading more than two feet of snow in an afternoon. The snowfall that followed was less severe, but enough to maintain rolling drifts and an eerie white calm.

3. New Year's Eve. I was standing at a window in the great room. From where I stood, I could see the glow of the post-lights scattered along either side of the drive, marking where the white surface of the drive ended, and the white surface of the park began. The snow was falling again, burying traces of bird-foot and animal-paw. It clung to the upper side of the branches of the maple trees, the silver-grey bark still exposed below.

I thought I saw a flash of something moving between the trees, a vivid red. I leaned into the glass to take a closer look. Nothing. Frozen trees and pristine snow. Denise came over to see what I was doing.

'I thought I saw something out there, something red,' I told her, 'a vivid red.'

'Probably a bird.'

We stood there for a moment, shoulder to shoulder, looking out the window into the darkness. Like a couple from a distant time, posing for a portrait. It felt strange for us to be standing so close together. No longer familiar.

'How is the work coming along?' Denise asked.

'Slowly. I feel like I am walking in circles, repeating everything I have done before.'

Denise didn't reply but I could sense her reaction, needle-like crystals interlocking and spreading out, cementing an icy status quo. I wondered why she asked the question if she could not bear to hear the answer.

I decided to change the subject.

'I had that dream again.'

'What dream?'

'I told you.'

'Maybe you shouldn't sleep during the day.'

4. I went to the kitchen to get some ice. A small TV, inset into one of the shelves, was flickering in the dark. An airborne camera panning over a frozen sea of ice, a glimpse of sunlight on a silver wing. National Geographic. A warm English voice narrating, a voice from my childhood. *Here in this white desert, life hangs in suspension, in what was once the mythical land of Ultima Thule, the most northerly region of the known world, beyond space, and beyond time.*

I walked into the pantry and opened the chest freezer and pulled out a bag of ice-cubes and looking down into the blue, frozen cavity, I thought, not for the first time, that even if we dream of the extremes, life is mostly lived in the middle.

When I returned to the kitchen Denise was there, barefoot on the cold stone floor, pointing a remote control at the little TV, skipping backward through the channels as if she was looking for something she had lost.

'I was trying to get the weather on cable. I can't get online, the connection's down. I think it's the snowstorm. I was wondering if Cassie's flight is going to be delayed.'

'You are worried about what is happening with the planes.'

'One can't help worrying about the planes Jerome,' she replied.

'In any case, whatever is going on with those planes has nothing to do with bad weather,' I said.

Denise smiled an irritated smile which said, 'you don't have any idea what you are talking about.' The phone in the hallway began ringing.

5. That Christmas I spent a great deal of time in my study doing very little work. Most of the time I stretched out on the chesterfield—a monstrosity in mahogany and oxblood leather which sat in the corner of the room— and drifted in and out of sleep. (The analysis couch Denise called it because she used to come in while I was working at my desk and stretch out on it and tell me her problems. But that was before. Denise no longer came into my study).

For a short time after waking, I would exist only as an abstraction. Without memory, without context. Often, as I surfaced, even when I remembered who I was, the context would continue to elude me. I was never quite sure if I was waking up in the cottage in the hills above Haven, or my bedroom in the house in Chorlton, or my mother's house in West Linn, or right here in Darkwood. And even when I understood that I was at the farmhouse, I would not be immediately aware of when. Of course, this uncertainty dissipated, but occasionally it seemed to me that there was something to exploit in a gap like that, an opportunity for change, a chance to do things differently, and I tried to prolong the feeling by resisting my return to full awareness. But it was not, ultimately, something I could control.

6. It wasn't new, this daytime somnolence. It was an old habit, but after what happened with William it took on a new urgency. Before it was an idle pleasure, later, sanctuary.

Before, I might have awakened to the sound of music and the high-toned ping, bright and pure, of a bar-spoon against the curved crystal walls of an old-fashioned glass. Denise might be preparing a cocktail. Perhaps she is arranging thin slices of an iridescent delicacy on a pair of plates—scallop or tuna—dotted here and there with sprigs of watercress, thin wedges of lemon. I walk down the hallway. I hear Etta James singing

'Stormy Weather' on a local radio station that liked to roll back a few decades after six p.m. each Saturday night. Denise looks up as I enter and notices that I have been sleeping again and hands me a drink and calls me Rip van Winkle. But that was before. The hallway is dark. The kitchen silent. Denise is in her study working, as usual.

These days I stop in front of the large gilt-framed mirror hanging in the hallway. I am not sure what I expect to see. Umber skin, black hair, thick but shorn tight, bright blue eyes. My father's skin, my mother's eyes. In my white shirt, standing in that checkered hallway I seem to hang there in that other world, as if I was a pale ghost, haunting myself.

7. It was traditional for couples to spend Christmas together—we had nowhere else to go. And so, we spent it together.

8. That Christmas, twin sisters in their early twenties were fatally wounded by a bullet that strayed from the crossfire of rival gangs. They were leaving a restaurant around 10:30pm. The restaurant was a French-style bistro; large windows bordered for Christmas with tiny white lights. Shots were fired. The sisters fell to the ground. One of the windows shattered, people began screaming inside, tables covered in white tablecloths tipping over as diners leaped from their chairs, a mirror cracked from side to side. Two sisters caught up in something that had nothing to do with them. Random, unpredictable. Shot down by a single bullet.

This happened in Manchester, England, where I once lived with my father through ten cold, wet winters.

9. That Christmas about two hundred people died when a cyclone hit an island nation in the Caribbean. The government was corrupt, and the island was bankrupt, so nobody sent in aid, at least at first, and when they finally did—after considerable pressure from celebrities grandstanding on social media—it was too late. In any case, these storms seemed more and more frequent. And what was one more storm?

It was only later, after seeing perhaps six different reports on this story, that I realized that the island was where my father was born.

10. That Christmas another plane went missing. A fully subscribed inter-national flight with 250 or so passengers lost contact somewhere over the Indian Ocean and disappeared, literally, off the face of the earth. The world had become so crowded, so known, every inch surveyed. When, a few years back, the first plane had gone missing, we huddled around our

screens, scarcely able to believe that such a thing was possible. A whole passenger jet melting into thin air. And each time it happened, it seemed, once more, newly impossible.

You can imagine the circus out there in the middle of the Indian Ocean, in the hot volatile winds spanning those old trade routes, ships of every imaginable kind lending a hand, searchers gazing down past the blue water into the dark trenches far beneath, lonely and secret corridors that perhaps granted passage to unknown worlds.

Another plane vanishing, beyond what we knew, beyond what we could understand, while we looked on in amazement, stuck to this damp, spinning rock, a rock which had got just a little bit bigger, once again.

11. That Christmas, forest fires continued to rage up and down the west coast. But there were so many other disasters happening that the longer they burned the less interest people seemed to have. The fire in the Haven hills had by then been contained. Malachy's 'villa' had been spared, as had most of Alain's vast estate, though one of his wineries had been damaged and he had lost many hectares of vines to the blaze. But it was the missing plane that interested me most. I read every article, watched every report, and even when they became repetitive, and there was nothing new to learn, I kept clicking and scanning and watching.

As with the previous plane, with no leads on what had happened, the side-show became the main event. The families were looking for answers. They stormed the press conferences and made demands online as people recorded them on their cell phones and shared them on their feeds. *We can't continue with our lives,* they said. *We cannot mourn our loved ones without bodies, without explanations. We need answers. We don't know how to go on.*

Denise appeared in the doorway (she always just materialized, no warning that she was en route). I pretended not to notice the way she looked at the bottle of bourbon on my desk, the rocks glass beside it with its generous double pour.

'The world is falling apart,' I said to her, 'we should expect a plague of locusts or blood falling like rain.'

'The world has always been falling apart,' Denise replied.

We stood watching the footage together for a moment. A group of protestors stood on a windswept beach at the edge of the sea, presumably in the region of one of the searches. People kneeling, howling in pain, their closed fists raised to the sky. A man struggled to hold up a cardboard sign bearing the words: 'Cannot mourn, cannot bury. Where is my son?'. The coastal wind hammered the mike-boom.

'Like Elpenor,' Denise said.

12. I kept reading. I kept watching. I worked back and read everything I could find on the previous plane. It was no longer just a discrete event; it was a phenomenon. It was a phenomenon that made me hungry for knowledge in ways I could not understand. Or perhaps I was just bored. I was no longer sure I could tell the difference.

MÓNICA PARLE

The Girl in the Glass House

Synposis

The Girl in the Glass House *is a coming-of-age literary novel set on the US-Mexico border during the ten most tumultuous years in borderlands history.*

Northern Mexico, 1913. Twelve-year-old Luz Carbajal's life is shaped by her glass-maker father, etiquette-obsessed aunt, feminist-anarchist mother, and brutal grandfather, who wrangled their land from the desert and its people.

Luz yearns for adventure off the hacienda, but her wish is granted in the worst way: after a disagreement, her grandfather disowns them. Emboldened by his absence, revolutionaries sack the estate leaving Luz the sole survivor. She vows never to forgive her grandfather.

Wracked with grief, Luz joins the flood of refugees headed to El Paso, Texas, where she meets the Olivas, a hard-working family hell-bent on vanishing into the melting pot. She clings to the new life they offer, battling segregated schools and humiliating work conditions.

But Luz soon discovers her body has stopped growing, and she fears her strangeness will thwart the Olivas's 'American Dream.' She goes it alone, eventually carving a life in a popular local vaudeville theatre, playing a never-ending roster of child characters. Still she doesn't grow.

To spur her body's clock, she resolves to make peace with her past and confronts her grandfather, but tormented by his own failures and suffering dementia, it's clear he can't offer Luz the closure she seeks. Just as she's leaving, his maid reveals a tantalizing secret: each week he's visited by a woman calling herself his daughter.

Luz discovers her mother survived, and has watched Luz's successes from afar, feeling Luz was better off without her. Overjoyed to be reunited, but wary of how they've both changed, they resolve to get to know each other as they are now. With her blessing, Luz embarks for the fledgling Mexican talking-picture scene in Hollywood.

Chapter 1

Even the heavens knew it was a special day.

After weeks of lead skies, twelve-year-old Luz Carbajal woke to the long-lost sun, glinting from the slit below her drapes. She tossed her blankets and ran to look. A wobbly yellow in a brittlebrush-blue that stretched for miles. Not one cloud from this window to the edge of the world! Why, even in China, they'd be gawping up at the same sky.

She smooshed her nose on the glass, looking out at the tufts of burnt grass spearing the sandy dunes and the creosote bushes that splayed in fans. In the orchard, bare branches scraped the sky, and the mountains on the horizon were a finger-print smudge of purple and blue. Her breath bloomed on the window.

Downstairs, her great-aunt Pola charred poblano chilies on the *comal*. The bitter smell tugged at Luz's nose. Poblanos were harvested come fall, and they were the only good thing about these months—well, those chilies and Mamá's birthday. The party was all they'd talked about for weeks, and now it was finally here. You had to dance for joy. Pola was cooking, the sun was out, and Luz had the *perfect* gift for Mamá.

She pulled her thick wool socks pulled up to her knees and raced downstairs, jumping from the third-to-last step and running into the kitchen.

'The sun's out!'

Pola's crossed gaze didn't waiver from the range. 'Bone cold, though. Worst possible day for a picnic.' She tutted. '*Madre de Dios*, what were we thinking?'

The first rule was not to let Pola's gruff ways chafe. 'Not *the* worst.'

'The sky's no better than dirty dishwater.' She nodded toward the table. 'Your *avenita's* long cold. Eat so I can clear it. Everyone else up for hours, and you, lolling in bed 'til noon.'

That stung. 'But Abel didn't leave me any lessons.'

'Lazy bones.'

It wasn't clear whether Pola meant Luz or her tutor, Abel. Probably, she meant both. Abel had gone home to the States nearly a month ago, and just hadn't come back. That hadn't sat well with Pola, but then nothing he did sat well with her.

No cross words nor spoonfuls of cold gruel would sap Luz's vim. Her feet jittered under the table, while she watched Pola flipping each chili back and forth over the flame, 'til the skin bubbled black with blisters. Pola's head tilted at an eternal angle, to give her good eye sight of a task. She slipped the charred chilies one-by-one into a hemp bag, tucking the booty tight to let steam separate the skin.

Luz kissed her fingertips, then raised them toward Pola's back in silent salute. *Chiles enogada* beat it all—poblano chilies crammed with Chihuahua cheese and beef, slathered in a sweet walnut sauce, and topped with pomegranate. How could they fail to please Mamá?

'Where is she?'

'In her study,' Pola's voice was thick with concentration. The chilies demanded it: they were prone to tearing in the fire. 'God help me,' Pola hissed as one did just that, and she scraped the precious flesh into a scrap basket by the sink. The *chachalacas* would feast tonight. 'What a waste.' Pola's lips went on whispering silent curses.

It was hard not to take this as a sign. 'Please make it go well.'

'What's that?' Pola's tone was all last straw.

Luz fiddled with her spoon. 'Papá, I said. Where's he?'

'At the *taller*.'

Pola needn't have answered. No matter the hour, or the day, Mamá and Papá would be sure to be found in their roosts: Mamá in her study and Papá in his glass workshop. Now and then Mamá ventured to town for supplies, but mostly Luz's parents clung to their quarters like those pigeons Abel talked about, the ones with an born instinct for flying home. But Luz asking was as much a part of her morning as polishing her teeth or putting on shoes. She was liable to fall down dead if the answer changed.

'May I be excused?'

Pola's mouth dropped open. 'You ate faster than a dog.' She pointed the sharp edge of the tongs, eyebrows arched. 'You'll choke if you're not careful, and that'll be the death of you.'

Luz looked cowed as she could. But Pola's bossing was always peppered with threats of death, and they'd long ago lost their sting. Once Pola's back was turned, Luz swabbed her face clean and threw the napkin on the table.

'Just a minute, señorita.' Pola narrowed her eyes. 'You sound hoarse.'

Luz backed toward the door. 'I'm fine.'

Pola scoured her hands, and it was a wonder she had any skin left after a scoring with that boar-bristle brush. She bid Luz come to stand before her, and Luz wriggled under Pola's scrutiny, but she kept her lips buttoned. No amount of harassing would hurry Pola. Vexation would only slow her down, and there was no chance of escaping this inspection.

Pola's hand was marble on Luz's forehead. 'The last thing we need is to spend the day fetching the doctor.'

Luz did her best to be the picture of health. Pola searched with her good eye for any sign of flu in flushed cheeks. It wouldn't be good to be too pink, or too pale, eyes too wet or too dry. Luz strived for middling in every way.

Pola's crossed eye seemed to pine for the back door. It'd been two years since she'd left the house, not since the dictator was ousted. She went only so far as the backyard when the weather was warm, and then only because hanging the laundry required it.

How terrible being shut in eternally would be. All that was exciting in the world lay out of doors, and even more so outside the hacienda gates. There was far too much in this world to explore. Why deprive yourself of even a second?

It was hard to imagine the child her great-aunt might've been. A dour girl, probably, one who preferred to spend hours re-rolling the socks in her drawers. Luz bit back a smirk at the thought of Pola tearing across the fields, skirts whipping and snagging on the tall stalks of grass. Pola's world was governed by dos and don'ts, and there seemed to be millions more on the second list than the first. Her great-aunt's frown deepened as if she could hear Luz's thoughts. And golly, you should put nothing past her. Luz straightened, smoothing the expression on her face.

Pola folded her arms over her chest. 'You can go,' she said, with a grudging sigh. The sweetest words in the whole world.

Luz crammed her socks into gum-boots. Tearing a shawl from a hook by the door, she pulled Papá's knit hat over her tangled hair and darted outside.

Pola's voice barked at her back. '*Dios mio!* You're still wearing your nightgown! I meant go get dressed, not straight out.'

But Pola wouldn't dare follow. Luz was safe as socks outside.

'You'll catch your death,' Pola shouted, before slamming the door hard enough to rattle the glass.

*   *   *

Fall's axe fell hard every year. True to Pola's word, a bitter wind nipped Luz's bare legs as she ran across the garden, but no matter: fall would take NO inch today. Time had crawled since she'd buried her gift, and it was all she could do not to dig it up every day to check it. Abel had made her swear not to—not before today.

Across the kitchen garden, then over the fence into the flower garden. Gray husks and withered stems cowered in what had been, just a couple months ago, a hubbub of pinks and purples, oranges, yellows, and blues. Now the dirt ruts had shriveled and the chalky caliche poked through.

Papá and Pola said Mamá especially suffered in fall. Heavens knew what really affected her. They never spoke of her malady. The little Luz knew came from half-heard words. Worse: everyone—Pola, Papá, the doctor—pointed to different proof.

Nervios, Pola called it. The affliction had come on violently, she said, but traces had always been there, starting with a stripe of stubbornness and single-mindedness in Mamá's childhood. Pola said that willfulness turned Mamá sour and mulish, but it was her time at school in Mexico City when it'd all gone wrong. If only they'd kept Mamá close, shown her how to devote herself to the care of others. Pola swore up and down they'd not make the same mistake with Luz.

'Tempers' was Papá's word. Mind you, rarely did he call it anything at all. For Papá's way was never to look a beast in the eyes. The doctor described Mamá's moods like a tornado, unpredictable and whirling, owing to the fact she had so little 'domestic occupation.' Left alone in her study, he said, dark thoughts gathered, then hurled out.

Still, the one thing Papá and Pola agreed on: fall's gray days were a trigger.

Today was their chance to make Mamá well again, but the garden was in fall's throes. Not for the first time, Luz wished she were a god. Not like the Greek gods in Abel's books, who clashed with lightning bolts and made the seas swallow towns. Or the gods of the Maya, who challenged heroes to play ball games in exchange for their lives. Or even Pola's god, who brought Jairus's daughter back from the dead.

No, what she asked for was just the teensiest of magic: a natural force. If only *every stitch of her* was filled with it. She'd be a god like her forebears, who with blood and sweat made crops and flowers grow in the desert. Then, she could make this day perfect for Mamá, and they'd be happy again.

She closed her eyes, picturing green shoots slinking beneath the earth, tunneling like millipedes. A curled stalk, tiny as her pinky nail, leaves and buds sprouting. Then the whole garden blooming: blackfoot daisies, purple sand bells, and red and pink trumpet lantanas. Firecracker bushes popping out in coral bursts. The *Lluvia de oro* trees with their green stockings and fringed yellow gowns. Life so thick it caught in your lungs like pollen.

She summoned all the wishing, hoping, and praying she could muster. Now, finally, the gods themselves would smile on them. One, two, three ...

Nothing. The grass was stiff with frost, leaves and dead stalks drooping.

What on earth was she expecting? This was just a child's game. Magic was the stuff of stories, not real life. She was just an ordinary girl. Papá and Pola reminded her fifteen times a day, when she stayed out too long in the garden, or she asked too many questions, or she wanted to help in the *taller*. Their words hissed in her head: *You're just a girl. Just a girl.* Again and again, until she had to press her hands to her ears and tuck her head between her knees to make it stop.

She walked on to the forked Elder in the corner of the garden. It had tentacled roots that shot up from the soil and then curled back underground. The hatches of a bobcat's claws lurked at the base of the tree, but from the thickness of the brittle grass, her hidey hole hadn't been mussed. She lowered to her belly and wedged her arm into the hollow underneath.

It'd been so cold over the last few weeks. Her only hope was that the cotton had kept the butterfly safe. It had to be fate that made her see it skimming over the wildflowers last month. The idea had come from Abel's lessons. All summer, he'd been singing the praises of conservation: they'd read of Darwin's voyage collecting specimens on the Beagle and the US President Roosevelt's expedition to Africa. These extraordinary men had voyaged to places unknown and brought back incredible finds to show for their toils. Abel had *tears* in his eyes when he talked about the American bison. One day they'd exist only in legend, and what trace would they leave once they'd vanished? The pelts and specimen great men collected would ensure they lived forever.

It was a short skip to wonder what would vanish from this land of theirs? The question hit Luz with a thump. What trace would be left when Mamá, Papá, and Pola were gone? Even now, her chest hurt to think it.

Her favorite species they studied by far was the Monarch butterfly, which traveled thousands of miles, from Canada all the way across the Chihuahuan Desert, before heading on to the Selva Lacandona farther south. That a wisp of a thing could weather rains and wind on such fragile wings! At night she'd pored over the atlas, tracing the route from Montreal, her finger drifting over places she'd only read about: Michigan, Indiana, Illinois, Missouri, Oklahoma, and Texas.

Surely, a monarch would be the perfect gift for Mamá. Not only was the butterfly beautiful, but it possessed such a fierce spirit, and that spirit could stay with them forever.

For weeks, Luz had waited, but by late September, they'd still not come. Maybe the Monarchs avoided Mexico along with the other North American tourists. Then one day, she lay in her secret creek, and a black-orange speck appeared in the sky.

It'd been so easy: the Monarch kept extra still on the purple milkweed. She caught it in her skirts, clutching the linen tight, and she swore she felt its wings beat at her belly. A jar of chloroform was waiting on the schoolroom shelf. She tipped the butterfly inside, but once it started twitching, she couldn't bear to watch. She'd fled to her room and hid under her bed til dinner. A dusty cast of its wings had imprinted on her skirt.

Abel had pulled the dead butterfly out so gently the next day. Who knew his chorizo fingers could be capable of such tenderness? Mostly, he was bull-headed, not given to a wick of kindness.

Her heart had thrummed as she'd watched. What would death look like? How strange that the butterfly looked much as it had alive. Abel showed her how to pin its thorax to the cork, spreading its wings without flaking off any more scales. They'd laid it to rest in the can on a bed of mothballs. Abel had scoffed at her offer of a prayer, but it felt wrong to bury it without, so she whispered one when she put it here in her secret spot.

Her fingers crept deeper, fumbling until they brushed metal. She drew the coffee can out, holding her breath as she removed the cotton. Her skin tingled at seeing those wings as vivid as before. How she longed to feel its scales ruffle, but she didn't dare. She sat back against the tree, closing her eyes. All would be well. Just as in fairytales, the spell over Mamá would be broken.

MATTHEW PUTLAND

SOLAR

Synopsis

SOLAR *is a Young Adult novel inspired by realistic predictions of how future space agencies would respond to an asteroid threat.*

In the year 2030, an interstellar asteroid named Viatrix is detected entering the outer reaches of the solar system. Its appearance triggers the formation of ICERN, a collaboration of the five largest space agencies in the world.

Seven years later, the mission is fully underway, with a revolutionary new asteroid diverting strategy called SOLAR. This system requires a constant crew on Mars as the first responders to the threat. Amongst the crew is Alex Rosegreen, software engineer and astronaut.

Unbeknownst to the world, when SOLAR fails to divert Viatrix, ICERN propels project Obsidian to the forefront of their agenda, having to tiptoe around diplomatic treaties and freedom of information acts.

Back on Earth, Alex's husband Nathan is starting to get nervous. Their sixteen-year-old daughter Aurora, and soon to be formally adopted eleven-year-old son Charlie, experience unnerving changes at school that soon escalate out of control as the world begins to suspect that the asteroid is still on its way.

Tensions heighten when the family receive a government alert to relocate to Bunker 37. The only problem is that Charlie isn't given a ticket.

Thrown into a perilous journey, the Rosegreen family must overcome lawless citizens, blackouts and meteor strikes, alongside trying to devise a plan to get Charlie inside the bunker with them.

When all seems lost, a last-ditch attempt by ICERN proves successful, saving the Earth but diverting Viatrix towards the moon. Both bodies are destroyed, leaving Earth without its closest neighbour. Now the world will have to recover from the mass hysteria of the asteroid and a planet without its moon, which turned out to influence more than just the night sky.

Chapter 1

Inverness 2037

Come on, you can do this, it's a good job.

Chidi forced himself to keep staring into the mirror. No, he had to let it go, he couldn't continue to mope about his car crash of a career. He just had to pay his time in this dump and then he might be able to get back on track. With *his* scores they'd be mad to waste him here.

'Sorry to rush you Chidi, but your shift starts in seven minutes,' rang a voice throughout the room.

Chidi turned back to his bed. It was only three steps from his bathroom mirror, one if he lunged. The entire room was in fact barely ten metres long and just over an arm's width wide. He'd been cooped up in here for five months now, and it was clear by the state of the room.

Chidi liked to think he kept things tidy, but the mess had gradually crept up on him. Dirty clothes were piled near the washing basket, empty plates from the night before were still strewn over the desk. The only thing that looked as fresh as the day it had arrived was his monitor that doubled as his television, it sat above the desk on the wall, an old 2030 model but perfectly functional. The internet on site was slow but managcable – thankfully, he'd quickly learnt that by switching his other devices off, he could get a reasonably good service.

Over the past few months, he'd gotten into a bit of a routine, he liked hearing the BBC News stream in the morning, it kept him connected to the rest of the world, a tall feat considering where he was.

Grabbing his last ironed shirt from the wardrobe and chucking the coat hanger onto his bed, he caught the tail end of the news report.

'*Breaking news this morning, the first close up photograph of asteroid Viatrix goes viral, captured by the Mars Huygens telescope. The astonishing image shows the true size and appearance of the asteroid, allowing scientists to analyse its composition in greater detail. The interstellar asteroid, which made headlines five years ago when it entered our solar system, has now reached the main asteroid belt just beyond Mars. Current ICERN simulations suggest it will travel past the Earth at a relatively safe distance in two months' time, posing a spectacle not seen for millions of years. Scientists are keen to take this opportunity to collect samples from the interstellar traveller, with Professor Heike Bartal joining us this morning.*'

'Chidi, you now have four minutes until your shift starts,' came a voice from the speakers. 'You really don't want to be late again.'

Chidi snapped away from the TV. 'Thanks Rider,' he said, fumbling with his shoelaces as he stumbled towards the door. 'Turn everything off will you.'

'Will do,' said the voice.

Slamming the door behind him, Chidi made a dart down the corridor towards the stairs. Why did he always do this to himself, Murray was just looking for a reason to demote him to desk duty- the boredom would be murder.

Climbing the steps three at a time, Chidi flung open the metal door that had a spray-painted four in the centre and checked his watch. He still had a minute; with any luck he wouldn't even be late.

Slowing down his pace, he made a left. Rows and rows of offices lined the corridor, each one with its own complete fireproof door and bulletproof glass. Most of the rooms already had people inside, all looking up with interest as he made his way past.

24.B, 25.B, 26.B, here we are. Chidi paused, just out of sight from room 27.B. Checking his collar was straight and his shirt was tucked in, he glanced at his watch again. Ten seconds. Giving a thumbs up to the grey-haired man in the opposite office, who clearly found his appearance more interesting than his own work, Chidi stepped through the doorway.

'God damn it you're lucky Robinson, four more second and that would be it!'

'Morning Lieutenant Murray,' Chidi said cheerfully, taking in a quiet gulp of air. Blimey, he really needed to work on his fitness. In front of him were seven other people, all sitting on thin, uncomfortable fold out seats. They all swivelled and stared at him, a few with unapproving looks.

Standing in front of the large screen on the far wall was a small woman with auburn hair, neatly tied into a ponytail. She wore her army uniform even though they were only required to wear their division's polo shirt.

Lieutenant Murray glared at him. 'Four seconds to spare is as good as late in my books,' she said. 'Fortunately for you I'm a woman of my word, take a seat.'

Chidi quickly slid into the back row, next to a man called Jason. He was one of the few people who hadn't rolled their eyes at him.

'Even for you this is close,' he whispered.

'What time did you get here then?' Chidi asked under his breath. Jason was usually no better than he was.

'I was classy,' said Jason, who was watching Lieutenant Murray bring up the day's agenda on the screen. 'I got here with a minute to spare.'

'Now that Robinson has graced us with his presence I can continue,' Murray said, cutting off the conversation. She turned and swiped at the screen. 'Today's a big day so I need you all on your game. We've got Martin Parkinson from the Ministry of Defence arriving for inspections. I know you will all demonstrate the high standards we expect from this division.'

A hand rose from the seat in front of Chidi. 'Why is Parkinson coming Lieutenant. Surely they wouldn't do the inspections?'

Murray quickly shrugged off the question. 'It's classified and of no concern of yours Griffiths.'

The woman lowered her hand quickly.

'On your pads you'll find your morning and afternoon duties. Any concerns please come and see me.' With that Murray turned off the screen. That was one of the benefits Chidi couldn't fault her on, she didn't waste time with drawn out speeches.

Reaching into his bag, he pulled out his line pad. Clicking the button on the top of the thin strip, the screen unravelled and flexed into its rigid shape. Quickly logging into the app, he couldn't help but smile at his duty list. Jackpot!

'What have you got?' Jason asked, peering over Chidi's pad. 'I'm on rota B.'

Chidi raised his hand. 'Looks like we're stuck with each other all day then.'

Giving a not so subtle high five, Chidi looked back down at the duties. They were on perimeter and facility checks, that meant just patrolling the site, including outside.

'What are you two grinning about?'

Chidi looked up to see the smiling face of Idaa Laghari. She was kneeling on a seat in the row in front, her arms clasped around its back. Her hair, unlike Lieutenant Murray's, was jet black and hanging loosely over her shoulders. Chidi had never seen her tie her hair up if she could help it. She was wearing black rimmed glasses today that somehow made her stunning brown and amber irises even more vivid. Chidi remembered on the first day of meeting her how taken aback he'd been by her eyes. She'd wasted no time in bragging that she had heterochromia, a condition seen in only one percent of the population. Idaa had told him this before she'd even given him her name.

'What have you been landed with?' he asked, already tucking his line pad into his pocket.

Idaa flicked her head towards the woman who had raised her hand earlier. 'I'm on rota D with Grace.' Her expression suggested she wasn't too happy about the prospect.

'Have fun with that,' Jason said, grabbing his own bag and grinning. 'I did rota A with her last week, I learnt all about the different ways I could get court-martialled if she had the inclination to tell on me.'

Idaa smirked. 'Well, I'm an exemplary soldier, so I'm sure that was just for you.'

* * *

Five hours later found Chidi and Jason strolling into the restaurant. It was called that to apparently boost the experience, but it was in actual fact just an oversized canteen. It was low roofed and wide, with a capacity to feed over two thousand hungry residents. Not that it ever had that many, there were precisely thirty-eight people on site at any one time - the skeleton staff they called themselves.

Chidi was in good spirits as he queued for his lunch. He and Jason had spent a good three out of the five hours patrolling the recreation floor. They'd made sure to check that the basketball court, trampolines and gymnasium were in working order. He'd lost to Jason on the three-point shootout but managed to claw back a victory on the trampolines by pulling off a double somersault.

He saw Idaa, Grace and a woman called Francine chatting at one of the many empty tables. After waiting for Jason to pick the type of dessert he wanted, they made their way over, zigzagging between the tables and chairs.

Chidi's heart spiked slightly as Idaa looked up at him. She smiled whilst chewing on her spaghetti and corn meatballs.

'Been working hard?' she asked, grinning as he and Jason took two of the empty seats. Grace nodded at them both but didn't stop eating to talk. Francine hadn't even registered their arrival, continuing to stare at the flat screen on the far wall.

'You know us,' said Jason, placing his lasagne to the side and starting on his bread-and-butter pudding. 'Had to make sure the equipment wasn't faulty.'

Grace frowned at him, though still didn't say anything.

'How's your day going?' Chidi asked, skewering a corn meatball with his fork.

Idaa shrugged. 'All right, we met the Ministry of Defence person. Murray asked us to show him around the accommodation rooms and facilities. Then we had to wait for an hour while he went into a meeting.'

'What was it about?' asked Chidi. This was the first bit of gossip they'd had since arriving. Nothing worth noting ever happened.

'No idea,' said Idaa. 'They went into the control room so couldn't hear anything.'

'And you shouldn't have even been trying to,' said Grace, who seemed focused on getting the last bits of yogurt onto her spoon. 'It's classified for a reason.'

Idaa waved her hand. 'Come off it Grace, aren't you the least bit curious. Even Murray wasn't allowed in.'

Chidi looked over to Francine, her food had hardly been touched. She was just sitting, completely oblivious to the conversation. He suspected she hadn't even registered his and Jason's arrival.

Following her eyeline, he caught sight of the screen on the wall. It was showing more news coverage of that asteroid the BBC had talked about earlier.

'What do you guys think about this asteroid then?' he asked the table. 'Do you reckon it'll hit Earth?'

Jason shook his head before swallowing. 'Not a chance,' he coughed. 'It's just the media whipping up a frenzy.'

'I don't know,' said Idaa. 'It said this morning that ICERN was preparing SOLAR. That must mean it's on a trajectory towards us.'

'Do you want to bet on it?' said Jason, reaching his hand across the table. 'Ten pounds it will miss Earth.'

Chidi smirked. Trust Jason to turn an asteroid into a profit.

Idaa looked unsure. 'Wait, would you get the money even if SOLAR redirected it?'

'Well yeah, if it missed Earth,' said Jason, still keeping his hand outstretched.

'Then no,' protested Idaa. 'That's an unwinnable situation for me.'

* * *

An hour later, Chidi and Jason were making their way up the steps towards the South Entrance. The site had four points of entry, the East was the main entrance for arrivals, the West for deliveries and the North and South were backups. Every month the entrances had to be opened and closed for maintenance and checks. It would be rather problematic if they failed to open in an emergency.

Scanning his biometrics, the display on the wall changed to a code pad. Tapping in that month's code, he heard the bolts unlock and the suction of the vacuum layer fill with air. Every inch of the site that was above ground was reinforced with recycled metal, five inches of dirt and soil and a one-inch vacuum layer. It was well protected, but a pain to get out of in a hurry.

Once the first door opened, he watched as Jason started unlocking the second bolted door. This one was a lot quicker and in an instant Chidi experienced the wonderous sensation of a summers breeze. It stroked his face and arms as he took several deep breaths. He hadn't realised how stifling the recycled air was in comparison to the real thing.

Walking out into the daylight, Chidi's spirits lifted even further. He squinted as the sun glared down from a cloudless blue sky.

Either side of the entrance were heaps of earth, neatly compressed into hills that could be climbed. The entire facility in fact was within a deep mountainous area of Scotland, with steep hills that ran all around.

Chidi led the way as they started climbing up the incline. The man-made hills would bring them right on top of the building. Woodlands were dotted around either side of them, but apart from that their view was completely uninterrupted.

'Anyone there?' Jason asked a few steps behind.

Chidi poked his head above the peak of the mound but saw no one. 'All clear.'

Taking a seat on the top of the hill, he found himself surrounded by long yellow grass, overgrown from lack of maintenance. Chidi took out his flask and gasped as ice cold water met his lips. Just that small walk alone had caused him to sweat profusely. It may be September, but the summer heat was still raging with no sign of stopping for Autumn.

'Did you fill out the paperwork?' Jason asked, already lying flat on the shrivelled grass.

Chidi took his time answering. He looked into the distance between the two largest hills. There was a lake glimmering in the sun, so inviting in the heat. In their free time a lot of them would head down there for a swim. 'Not yet,' he said. 'I figured I've only got three more months left on my contract, then I'll see.'

'I don't know why you'd want to leave this place?' Jason said, his eyes shut. 'This is a great gig.'

Chidi shrugged. 'Aren't you bored of living in a bunker?' He glanced over to the deserted East entrance. 'I mean, what's the point of us even being here.'

GEMMA SELTZER

Me, Rosa and Bridget Bird

Synopsis

NELL, a woman in her late thirties, arrives unexpectedly at her older sister's home and refuses to leave. She and ROSA have not seen each other in five years.

Uninvited but undeterred, Nell moves into the spare bedroom and increasingly disrupts her sister's life. She wears clothes to match her little niece, grows wildflowers in soil she dumps in the room and shakes up Rosa's calm, ordered existence.

This is a contemporary literary novel, set in London. The chronology moves between the sisters' schooldays, their time as students and as young women and into the present day. The reader slowly pieces together the fragments of the story.

We learn the reason for Nell's erratic behaviour: she's grieving Bridget Bird, known as BIRD. Bird was Rosa's closest friend and – for many years – Nell and Bird conducted a secret friendship. Rosa's discovery of the clandestine relationship drastically changed the lives of the women, severing ties between them all.

The two estranged sisters are brought together by the news of Bird's sudden death and her presence haunts their reunion. They now must face the past and attempt to rebuild their relationship.

This is a novel that foregrounds women's friendship, which is often underestimated or ignored in cultural narratives. Typically, stories depicting women's relationships with each other focus on rivalry, a shared interest in seeking romance, or an intimacy that is later defined as sexual attraction or undeclared love.

'Me, Rosa and Bird' takes female friendship seriously and shows it as a sublime, foundational relationship for three women. The book also explores grief, Jewish culture and childlessness. For each of the characters, the friendship allows them to escape the confines of expected, traditional roles and to explore the deepest aspects of themselves.

Me, Rosa and Bridget Bird

NELL

From across the road, I watch my sister Rosa thread fairy lights through the branches of a silver birch tree. It's a cool December morning and the sun is weak in the sky. She's on a stepladder and the trail of lights hangs over her shoulder. Rosa winds the string around the white bark, slowly, as if she's wrapping a bandage.

This is where she lives, then. A neat semi-detached home, with a fenced garden circling it, like a moat. On her front door she's hung a massive wreath with berries and navy-blue ribbons. Inside, no doubt, she'll have carols purring and spiced candles flickering. The bag on my shoulder is heavy after the uphill walk from the station.

'We're Jewish, you know!' I yell from my piece of pavement to the tree she's decorating.

My sister turns. It's been five years since we've seen each other. When she rolls her eyes, I break into a smile. When she shakes her head and chucks the remaining fairy lights upwards into the tree, I laugh.

Inside, Rosa makes tea. Her hair is long, wound in a bun behind her ear. She's smart in slacks and a wispy blouse. While she reviews the inside of a cupboard containing tins in neat rows, I flick through the envelopes on the table. Christmas cards for various delivery people. My niece Franny's crappy drawings are on the front, plus a twenty-pound note. I take the money for the postman and stuff it in my pocket.

'I really wish you'd called, Nell. Franny's away this evening, at her friend's. I would've asked her to stay. I could've made up the spare room,' my sister says, pouring hot water into two china mugs.

'Yeah, sorry about that,' I reply. What I don't say is: *Asked* Franny? Asked? The kid is six years old. I look around. Antique sideboard with ceramic bowls and plates in boring colours. One pile of magazines and another of papers. Single cup drying on the draining board. Smug house plants with shiny leaves. I bet she has a cleaner.

Rosa sits opposite me, bringing a platter of fruit and cakes. 'Hungry?'

'Sure.' Without really thinking, I pick up some peach pieces and drop them into my hand. Then I decide against it and return the slices to the plate. 'Actually, no thanks.' I suck the stickiness from each of my fingers, one by one.

'Nell?' Rosa says.

'What?' I say, frowning. 'We've got the same germs.'

'Here.' She folds a napkin in front of me. 'I'm having a nightmare with Franny's school. I have to *assume* she's actually learning because there's no evidence of that from the teachers. One of the dads helps her with maths. Curtis.'

'Right.'

She continues, 'It's the subject I worry about the most. Maths was never my forte. She's with her friend tonight. Marnie. Curtis' daughter.'

'Marnie's a good name,' I say.

'They're like sisters. Franny and Marnie. Close, I mean. They spend a lot of time together.' Rosa pauses, then nods towards the plate. 'Try the sunshine muffins,' she says. 'They're vegan.'

I remember how my sister always slipped important news between other pieces of information. That was her habit, even as a child. I glance at the muffins, think about Franny, and then it dawns on me that Rosa must have a boyfriend. Curtis. Well, good for her.

'It's a nice road you live on,' I say.

Rosa stares out the kitchen window into her back garden. I look too. There's a shed painted a pale green colour. Plus a pond. A frog hops into view, then leaps out of sight. An actual frog. In South-East London. I wonder if her neighbours have seen it too. I hope they have and call my sister the frog-woman or croak when she passes.

'I could tell which house was yours,' I say and pick up my drink. It has a brisk, spicy taste and a nasty floral smell.

Rosa takes her cup and blows on its surface. 'Really?'

For a cautious moment we face each other, then we look towards the window again. I watch a squirrel pause by the foot of a tree. 'In your letters, I remember you bought a handmade mat for the toilet and it was rare and expensive.'

'Ha, do you?' Rosa says.

I want her to correct me and say it was not so expensive, or it was a bathroom rug, or an accent rug, or Persian carpet. But no, she says nothing. She definitely doesn't deny it. I say, 'You have style. You always had.'

Her eyebrows raise. She doesn't know what to make of me, but she accepts the compliment. 'I second guess myself. I always did. A lot more than I do now. But I still do.'

'You always knew exactly how things should be and when and where.' I pause. 'I used to make lists of your opinions.' I put my mug down. 'I wonder what they said? All I remember is you believed only stupid people used bookmarks. I almost failed exams for that one.'

'You're joking!' says Rosa. 'You always seemed...' She runs her fingers across the table.

An image from the past shoots into my mind, pulsing with detail. It's me, Rosa and Bridget Bird, who everyone called Bird. From the first week of Year 9 those two had become inseparable. In the afternoons, we all would sit at our kitchen table to snack on biscuits. Mum would be on the phone somewhere. Rosa and Bird would talk and talk and I would pretend not to listen.

The moment I remember is the time I sucked on chocolate digestives and opened my mouth for them to see. 'Look!' I said, then laughed and shook as if an electric shock passed through my body. Rosa turned to Bird. 'Gross. Can you imagine being friends with her?' Bird laughed. She could, definitely. 'What?' Rosa frowned. '*Actual* friends?' Bird shrugged. 'Really? Like, to go shopping and talk about things with?' I rubbed chocolate over my lips. 'Bit shocked to hear that,' Rosa said in a quiet voice. 'What makes you say so? She's too little to understand life, like *we* do.'

There was a three-year age gap and I was still extremely interested in the contents of the toilet bowl before I flushed. Bird was going to say I *was* too young, I *was* immature. But Bird was absolutely still. A strange quirk I later knew well: an ability to become statue-like. Her body hung for a moment like a question mark, and then she breathed out and said, 'Nell is fun.' Rosa reacted. '*I'm* fun!' Bird raised her eyebrows. 'I wouldn't exactly call you fun, Rosa.'

Bridget Bird shifted in her seat and faced me. Something unspoken travelled between us, back and forth. Bird put her arm around Rosa, squeezed her close and whispered into her ear, loud enough for me to hear, 'You have loads of other nice qualities, though. Loads.' Rosa blushed.

Bird picked up a biscuit, took a bite and winked at me. She then leaned over the table and opened her mouth to show a pulpy brown mess. I remember looking at the line her fringe made across her forehead, her tiny little teeth. I felt strange but I grinned. 'Disgusting,' I said. Bird chewed and smiled. Was that the moment? When I knew everything that happened next was inevitable?

I shake off the image and say to Rosa, 'Would you say you're well off?'

My sister turns to face me. 'Would I *say* so?'

'Sorry. You don't like to talk about money?'

Rosa shrugs. 'No, it's not…'

'Forget it. Forget I asked. You'll forget I'm here after a while.'

She chooses her next words carefully, as if guessing the answer to a crossword clue. 'You'll be…' she says. 'Staying?'

'Really? Thank you, I'd love to.' I smile. 'This tea tastes a bit funny, Rosa. Do you have any Coke?'

* * *

Mid-morning. I hear the doorbell chime and a blather of voices downstairs. I stretch out on my back. A refreshing night's sleep, like drifting along in a warm ocean. I remember the journey here yesterday, the walk from the station, the silver birch, the wellies, the walk in the woods with Rosa and finding the kitten under a fallen branch. I open my eyes and I remember my plans.

The wall clock shows twenty past ten. At least I think so, but the brushed brass clock face has been stripped of any actual useful details. No numbers or markers, only three arrogant hands ticking around a blank circle. I can imagine Rosa describing her purchase to her friends: *Time, but timeless.* Or, *Natural, honest materials.* And, *Clean lines, that appeal in this culture of sensual overload.* Blah, blah. I'm good actually. I'm getting the hang of Rosa.

I watch the clock. Footsteps dash on the wooden floor downstairs. Someone laughs. Has Franny now returned from her sleepover? Today's the day I'll see her. Not yet though as I'm too engrossed in this silky bed. Bamboo and microfibre duvet, Rosa told me last night. Very comfortable, very ethical. I arrange the blanket and lie perfectly still. This is a big room with three substantial windows. A wooden chair has a plumped cushion on its seat. A huge white paper star hangs from the ceiling.

What will I say to Franny? I'll speak to her about my life and tell her my side of the story. I'll tell her about other ways of living, with crap on the floor and wallpaper peeling. I wonder if she's ever even seen wallpaper? She might like me, but she might not. I have no idea what Rosa has told her about me, or what she's imagined.

Young girls always want someone unlike their mothers around, I know I did. My heart begins to assault my body with sudden heavy thumping, so I curl onto my side, thinking of Franny's face which looked from the photos I'd seen so much like Rosa's. A person with a tall, healthy, confident body that rises above all others. Rosa, her face like a prize, and she's passed that trait to Franny. The father's inferior genes couldn't fight the neat nose, good hair and such magnetism.

Stop feeling sorry for yourself. Bird isn't here and she won't be anytime soon. What's the use of thinking about her? She was Rosa's friend first, before she was mine. That's the simple story. I look around the room again. Yet another space in the house which has no colour.

Feet pummel on the stairs, then there's a squawking noise. My bedroom door swings open.

'Auntie Nell!' shouts Franny, jumping on the spot.

She has her hair braided into two plaits and wears a velour tracksuit which Rosa might say is a shade of earthy brown, and I would say is the colour of shit.

I turn my head on the pillow to face her. 'What?'

She claps her hands together. 'Thank you for the kitten! My mummy said you rescued it from under a huge tree.' Franny recites a streamlined version of the story in which Rosa and I coax the kitten out and there are no exchanges in which one of us invalidates the other's feelings with an eye roll. There is no mention of our jibes or Rosa's attachment issues with her phone. Franny asks, 'Was the kitten really scared? What kind of noise was it making?'

I shuffle upwards and arrange myself to see her better. 'Mewing, mainly. Why don't you make a few sounds and I'll let you know which is closest to the kitten?'

Franny likes that and performs a whole series of barks and squeaks.

'That's almost it,' I say at one point. 'But louder.'

Her voice rises into every corner of my room. I think about my sister who paid the vet bill and for the kitten food, but refused to make a fuss about our ball of fluff with its stinky breath that I have named Halitosis.

'What's going on up there?' calls Rosa from downstairs. There she is.

'Nothing!' I call.

'Auntie Nell?'

'I'm busy.'

'We have over one hundred plants and a greenhouse with more plants, and in my bedroom, I'm growing a cactus with bunny ears.'

She's not wrong. Every room of Rosa's house has too many plants, and this one is no different. There's a yucca here in the corner, and a few others including one with a single plasticky red flower. 'I hope you water your cactus every day.'

'No! You only water them sometimes.'

'Who told you that?'

'Mummy.'

'She's lying.'

Franny looks like she isn't sure what to do with the information. She says, 'Can I come and sit on your bed?'

'If you have to.'

She bounces up on the bed and rolls onto her back. Feet in hands, she rocks side to side.

'Don't wobble the bed, it's making me queasy.' No one would be impressed if I released the contents of my stomach onto the sheets. 'I hated everything about school, what about you?'

'It's okay. We have to stand in a lot of lines.'

I laugh at that. 'Anything else?'

'I like my teacher. I like that we live nearby so when I leave school at 3.15pm, we get home at almost exactly 3.30pm.'

'That does sound exciting,' I say. 'I heard you love baking.' I'd spotted a toy kitchen in the real kitchen yesterday. A dark rose wooden unit, with beige hobs and knobs and a fancy glass-fronted oven. There was an actual sink with a tap you lift, and a cupboard with a pale pink curtain swept across. 'You do know that thing you have by the dresser isn't real, though?'

Franny laughs. The dials turn, she's thinking, there are spatulas and lights. What's not real? 'I wish I was a fairy and could magic my mum to stop telling everyone how much I like baking,' she says. 'Life would be a lot easier.'

I look at her and wonder what it's like to be her. Nice toys and a big house. Clever, popular, an only child.

'I like your pyjamas, Auntie Nell.'

I look down at myself. The pyjamas have navy blue with stars, many moons and every planet in the solar system. Crimson piping trims the collar and buttonholes. 'Well, it's funny you should say that, because I brought you a matching set.'

'You didn't! For me?'

'For you.' I step out of the bed and head to my bag, which I tossed into a corner last night. 'Hope you like them.' I keep my tone even, as if none of this matters.

I bought the pyjamas in a shop by the station, next to the deli and the washing up liquid refill store. You'd imagine they'd smell of cellophane or dust, but the shop must have sprinkled them with lavender. The pyjamas were meant to be a joke, but they also represent the most serious thing I'd ever done.

Bad Luck Face

Synopsis

*On paper, **Kiran Aujla** is the very picture of a modern, liberated British-Asian woman – she's an Arts graduate, she has her own flat in Leeds, has recently been handed a promotion at work, lives far from her family in the Midlands, and is under no pressure to get married – she has it all. Or does she?*

*Bad Luck Face is a coming-of-age commercial novel set in 2005, following 23-year-old **Kiran** who returns to her hometown following the death of her grandmother, the controlling **Gurmit Kaur**. Her father **Tej** has unexpectedly sold the house and even more unexpectedly, has asked his daughter to help with the clear-out.*

It's only when Kiran comes back to West Bromwich, that she is forced to confront the true reality of her life – in her five years away, she has made no friends; her rented one-bed flat sits above a kebab shop; despite an Arts degree, she's the assistant-manager of a candle-store; she has never had a romantic relationship; she doesn't want the promotion she's been handed but is too scared to turn it down; and she's under no pressure to marry because she's estranged from her wider family after leaving for university and causing her grandmother's subsequent ill-health. If her father hadn't been the one to orchestrate her move away, she would never have left at all.

*In the two weeks she is home, Kiran is forced to face how much her mother's suicide when she was eight has impacted the decisions she has made (or rather, not made) in her life. Through a chance encounter with her mother's best friend **Hina**, forging a bond with Canadian student **Roop** and discovering her mother's lost letters, by the end of the novel, Kiran is stepping off a plane in Uzbekistan.*

Chapter 1

'And I suppose he's told you where his new place is?' Her aunt's eyes bore into her with uncomfortable intensity.

It was only now that Kiran remembered how her father had gripped the steering wheel when she'd asked, even though he'd been driving on an empty residential street. He didn't answer her question. Not that she'd really cared. She'd been too distracted by the undeniable fact that a part of her – tiny, hidden but most definitely there – was glad to be back.

Chapter 2
45 Minutes Earlier

The first thing Kiran spotted when she got out of the car was the SOLD sign tucked behind the black outdoor bin. She wished she could have seen it upright. Maybe then all this would have felt more believable.

The house looked bigger than she remembered. It's paint, once a garish blue, was peeling off in haphazard waxy patches. The windows gave off an algae-green tinge, while the frames were swollen and cracked, ready to abscond with the first invitation from a medium-force gust of wind. Water from a broken gutter under the roof dib-dabbed onto a spot on the second step which led up to the front-door.

Despite its dilapidated state, Kiran was envious of the house. In fact, she was envious of most buildings – their bulk, their patterned brickwork, their roofs holding them down, their straight lines, up down, across. No matter what, they always knew where they stood.

'It always does this.' Her father gave an embarrassed laugh as he pushed against the door with his left shoulder and twiddled the key with his right hand. 'It's like it never wants me to come in.'

'She's dead.'

The flat delivery of these two words last month had, for a second, made Kiran wonder whether she'd ordered a hit.

Her father didn't stop for breath during the seven-minute phone-call. There'd been so much to sort out once he'd found 'The Body'; the ambulance ('Which clearly wasn't needed'), the police, the coroner and of course, Gindi. Then the mourners began to arrive. While 'The Body' was still in the house, he'd practically shrieked.

'When will the funeral be?' she'd asked the first chance she was able to.

Silence.

Clearing of throat.

When he did answer, it was as though he was reading a pre-prepared script. 'I'm not sure yet. I'll have to check when the funeral lot can slot her in. Are you thinking of coming?' he'd asked tentatively, as though he'd feared putting the idea into her head even though she'd been the one to ask.

'Maybe I sh–'

'It's such a long way for you. No-one will expect you to be there. Best leave it, eh?'

A light breeze carrying summer away whipped around Kiran's shoulders as she took in her familiar surroundings. The street still looked the same, with its array of net curtains and stingy front gardens. Turner's Hill rose high behind the roundabout at the bottom of the road, its two radio transmission towers standing side-by-side like a bionic man-and-wife.

She looked across the road at Mr Dixon's house. His front-garden had once been the most colourful on the street, lace-edged petunias with amethyst hearts and shooting-star fuchsia's bordering an acid green stamp of grass every summer. Now dense weeds and overgrown bushes peeked over the low wall. With his uniform of three-piece-suit and pork-pie trilby, Abraham Dixon had lived opposite them for as long as Kiran could remember but she couldn't recall any of the Aujla's ever talking to him, a slight nod of the head the most that was given and received. Yet the absence of meaningful contact didn't stop him from being in the background of so many of her few memories, the tap-tap of his walking-stick providing a comforting, if one-note, soundtrack.

Turning back, Kiran found her father still pressed up against the door of the house he'd lived in for over four decades and which he'd sold only a few days after the funeral. He'd sounded jittery when he rang to tell her, like she was going to tell him off or something.

'You can come back and sort out what you want to keep. Or not. You might not want to bother. I just thought I should ask. You'll have to come soon if you do want to come. Or I can just chuck it all? That might be for the best.'

He gave the door one last shove. Finally relenting, it easily gave way causing him to go flying into the darkness of the hallway.

Kiran hesitated before making her way up the five steps. She wondered (as she'd done numerous times since last week) why she'd agreed to help clear the house.

And so readily.

The sparse light scattered as soon as Kiran closed the door behind her. She nudged her shoes off, surprised her father hadn't removed his.

It was as though she was stepping onto a well-observed film-set. Everything looked the same but just a little more worn – the blue vinyl running the length of the hallway to the kitchen; the magnolia banister leading upstairs; the wood-framed mirror whose edges had melded with the wall long ago. If anything or anyone had changed, it was her father, who disappeared into the sitting-room with what seemed to her to be a newly discovered lightness.

When he'd pulled up outside the tram stop, she'd expected to see the stress of the last few weeks on his face. Maybe a few worry lines across the forehead or fuller pouches under his eyes. Instead, he'd seemed *almost* giddy, as though his new (and questionable) stubbly beard was also imbuing him with a new personality. When he'd suddenly mentioned that he'd be shaving it off soon, the timing of the comment had taken her aback because they'd never been close enough for that kind of synchronicity and for it to start now, after five years of not seeing each other, was somewhat unexpected.

Placing her backpack onto the floor opposite the front-room, she looked inside at the two seaweed-green sofas, the ceramic figurines lining the window-sill and mantelpiece, and the four faded prints of native English flowers on the chimney breast. Her father had painted over the wallpaper in the late 80s, a small decorating victory for him until he realised the cerise and red damask design needed at least four coats of emulsion to cover it. He gave up after two, his depleted effort leaving behind baby-pink blooms which peeked out nervously from under the cream fog like shy bruises.

A large, gilt framed picture of the Golden Temple sat angled on the wall to preside over the lack of proceedings in the room. Thin velveteen curtains, which had once been sandy-gold, were now weary-brown. Net curtains, tinged yellow by the aging combination of condensation and sun, huddled together at the window to prevent outside eyes from peering in. The carpet, with its livid whirls of reds and browns, glared at her accusingly.

Thickly painted cream cabinets sat either side of the chimney breast. Behind their glass doors was the rhythmic display of drinking vessels. Each of the three shelves displayed a green tumbler, peach-lustre teacup down-turned on its saucer and a whiskey glass with the same pride an athlete might exhibit their medals. The memory of cleaning each of these items every Saturday morning to ready it for the visitors who rarely came, made Kiran's stomach twist sharply.

She looked down at her feet. This was where she'd been standing when the Doric column that had been her grandmother spat out the last words she ever spoke to her – 'Never come back'. As she'd absorbed the blow of that final command, a part of her had wanted to turn away from the open door and tell the unmoving figure that she didn't want to go, couldn't say what had come over her to think she could but that choice melted into nothing when she turned and saw her father in the driver's seat, his eyes imploring her to get in.

It took Kiran a few moments to realise that the sitting-room was now fully transformed into her father's bedroom. He'd always slept here, but by the time she came down in the mornings, he'd erased all signs of his overnight occupation. But today, the settee remained flattened out. A thin, bobbled sheet was spread over the dark settee cover while a pillow and duvet was shoved against the wooden arm-rest. Sat next to it on the floor was her grandmother's mahogany-varnished stool. On top was a half-drunk glass of water and on the floor, a heavily thumbed copy of an old Radio Times.

Kiran had never seen her father's presence in the house as clearly as this ramshackle display. His domain had always been the shop, a place she had little to do with. Unlike other shop-keepers whose families usually lived above their businesses, life swimming indistinctly around the two places, her father had been exacting in maintaining a physical and meta-physical distance between his two worlds. Not that Kiran had minded. Growing up, she'd hated the place, the convenience store conveniently absolving him of all his other responsibilities.

The ten framed technicolour prints of the Gurus which used to cover the wall above the gas heater now sat stacked on the floor next to the TV cabinet. Only grimy outlines remained on the thick vinyl wallpaper. The landscape rectangle had been a picture of Guru Nanak Dev-Ji sitting cross-legged between his two companions, Bala and Mardana. The smaller box above would have shown all the Guru's faces encircling the Golden Temple. To the right of that, a teeming crowd looking on as the young sons of Guru Gobind Singh-Ji were bricked up alive.

Sitting down on the upright settee, she pushed aside a pile of discarded clothes with a finger while her father sat back on his bed-settee, propping himself up with an elbow. 'You should've left your shoes on. There's no point in keeping anything clean now. You want some tea? I've got quite good at making it since you've been away.'

'No thanks, Dad. I've stopped drinking tea to be honest.'

Before she'd left, Kiran had drunk tea every morning, even though she'd never really cared for it. Gurmit Kaur would brew it for close to an hour, before adding the sterilised milk, a bottle of which always sat on the kitchen counter. The result was a beverage as heavy as an evening meal.

'Ah, moved onto the coffee? I know that's what you students love doing, sitting around with lattes. I watch 'Friends', you know. That Joey.'

Kiran offered a weak smile while deciding not to remind him that she wasn't a student anymore and that none of the 'Friends' characters were either.

'How's Mr Dixon?'

'Abraham?' Her father sat up. 'Can you believe he's dead as well? Only a week after your Dadi. Actually, no-one knows for sure *when* he died. From what I've heard, he'd been dead for a few days when he was found.'

A hard pressure began to build-up behind her eyes. 'That's horrible.'

Her father leant forwards. 'It's the worst way to go. All alone. For days. Just rotting away. By himself.'

Shaking her head, Kiran glanced at the wooden sideboard. It used to contain her grandmother's red comb, her bottle of baby oil, and the nail scissors she used to trim her chin hairs. Whenever Kiran walked in on her attending to them in the hallway mirror, she'd slip the scissors into the sleeve of her cardigan with the agility of a seasoned illusionist.

Kiran now expected the cupboard to be housing her father's socks and underpants, which were presumably covering the only two photo albums that remained. One contained a handful of photos of her teenage father and aunt wearing itchy, lurid jumpers while the other comprised of black-and-white images of morose relatives, names of whom which had probably died along with her grandmother.

There were no photos of her.

ANNA SONNY

The Foundation of Everything

Synopsis

Daniel and Jada, two thirty-something strangers living in London, take an online DNA test and discover they are related. The novel follows the two cousins and their subsequent search to uncover the truth about their family history.

Daniel and Jada have no idea how they are related. Daniel was orphaned at a young age and Jada's father Eli, who has dementia, is presumed to be an only child. When Jada discovers that Eli has been making regular payments to a woman called Marcelle in St Lucia, she thinks the answers may lie there. Wanting to find out the truth before Eli deteriorates, Daniel and Jada decide to fly out to the island.

The search seems fruitless at first as friends and family are not forthcoming. When Daniel and Jada separate after an argument, Daniel meets Melissa, who is fearless and lives life to the full, and quickly falls in love. Meanwhile, Jada bumps into an old family friend, who reveals that her father and Daniel's father, Flex, are brothers. Flex is on the run after accidentally killing Marcelle's brother thirty-five years ago. Eli witnessed the incident but has kept it a secret to this day, to protect Flex.

Jada is conflicted about telling Daniel, but eventually shares the truth with him. Daniel is initially shaken but feels free finally knowing what happened. Though Jada tries to convince him to come back to London, he decides to commit to Melissa and stays in St Lucia. Jada returns home alone.

This novel deals with the connection between family and identity, and the experiences of navigating life in London as the child of first-generation immigrants from the Caribbean.

Chapter One

Daniel turned into the quiet residential street, lifting his hood up as protection from the cold. Winter's early darkness had claimed the sky and the streetlamps cast an orangey glow over the road. Daniel couldn't draw his eyes away from the double-fronted houses with their plush hedges and neat lawns – a nice change from the grey, narrow streets of East London. He wondered if he would ever be able to afford such a house in his lifetime.

He texted Rosa to let her know that he had just stopped to pick up a bottle of her favourite wine and was on his way to hers now, he was only a few minutes away. These small gestures always pleased her and he wanted her in a good mood. A sharp bark made him look away from his phone and he was surprised to see a small Yorkshire Terrier sniffing around his trainers with interest. The dog looked up at Daniel and yapped a greeting, standing on its hind legs in excitement. Daniel had never really been that into dogs but the welcome reception warmed him. He looked up, ready to smile at the lady holding the leash, but her eyes were taut with fear. She drew her dog away from him and hurried off, her long dark hair flowing behind her.

Daniel turned to his reflection in the car window next to him. The hood shrouded his face in darkness. His plan for the evening was to spend the night in watching a movie on the sofa with Rosa, so he had put on one of his favourite grey tracksuits and a casual black puffy jacket. Years of rugby training had made his shoulders broad and standing at six feet four, Daniel had always been the tallest in his class. Always the tallest. And always the only black student in the whole year. He had left his house feeling casual and comfortable but seeing his reflection in this suburban street made him feel uneasy. He could see another woman in the distance walking towards him, talking to someone on her phone. The desire to continue walking to his car propelled him forward but the desire to not frighten someone else away held him back with equal force. After a moment he sighed, lowered his hood and crossed the road.

He waited for the woman to pass and he crossed back again, relieved that she hadn't even noticed him. He climbed into his car, and had just switched on the engine when a sudden boom erupted from the lonely street. Daniel ducked in his seat. He could feel his car leaning to one side. He looked up and down the street. There was nobody around. What on earth was that? He stepped out of the car, seeing curtains twitch in the houses across the street and heads appear at the windows. He walked around to the pavement and saw that his back tyre had blown. He swore violently.

He squatted down and peered at the wheel of his car. There was a huge rip in the sidewall of the tyre and most of it had come off the wheel completely – there was no way he could drive it. He had only got the tyre a few weeks ago. He cursed the mechanic under his breath. How much was that going to cost him? He tucked himself back in his car to escape the chilly air and looked for the number of his insurance provider. Would Rosa even believe him if he told her he was running late because his tyre had blown while his car was parked? A quick internet search brought up some results of forums with stories of those who'd had similar experiences and it seemed the issue could be fixed without his car being towed away. He decided to speak to the insurers first to find out how long they would take to come out so he could let Rosa know what time to expect him.

Twenty minutes later he was still on hold with the insurance company. He had his phone on speaker in his lap and his fingers tapped a beat on the steering wheel. A distant siren became louder and more piercing. Blue lights flashed in Daniel's rear-view mirror. As the police van rounded the corner he wondered what possible crime could have been committed in this immaculate neighbourhood. Especially ones that required a whole unit like this. Although who knew what kind of corruption these bougie dwellings housed? It could be embezzlement. People always seemed to want more, no matter how much they had. He remembered the hushed voices in the staff room at one of his previous jobs, when the shop manager was taken away in handcuffs after stealing money from the cash register for months.

The low battery notification appeared on his phone, and not wanting to get cut off from the call, he went to fetch his power bank from his gym bag in the boot. The van skidded to a stop halfway up the street. Maybe it was something to do with drugs? Sometimes gangs from the city came to the suburbs or rural areas and used kids to deal drugs, squatting in empty houses or abusing the vulnerable.

The van door swung back and a dozen police officers descended on the street in full gear, with dogs and rifles. This must be serious. Daniel had seen the police dramas on TV, and he knew they didn't carry weapons unless they were apprehending someone with a gun. Was he in danger? He craned his neck to see which one of the houses they were going to burst into.

'Hello?' A tinny voice sounded on his phone.

'Yeah hi, my tyre has just blown and I'm stuck parked on a side street in…hang on…'

Daniel could see a policeman sprinting towards him like a bowling ball headed for a strike. He turned back to look behind him, confused.

'Don't move! Put your hands in the air!' he heard the officer shout.

Daniel turned back to see a gun pointing at him. He dropped his phone and heard the crack of the screen as it hit the ground. The small black hole at the end of the gun hooked Daniel's gaze and seemed to grow bigger, sucking his concept of time, sound and speech deep into it, until the police officers, the dogs and the street behind it all merged into a silent blur.

'I said put your hands in the air!' shouted the officer, gesturing with the gun.

Daniel's arms went up. He couldn't look away from the gun. 'What's going...'

'Where's the gun?' the officer cut in, amped up.

'What gun?' Daniel yelled. 'I don't have a gun!'

In a swift movement the policeman ran forward, spun him around and shoved him up against the car.

'We've had reports of a gunshot coming from this street and someone who fits your description acting suspiciously. Now tell me where the firearm is.'

A gunshot? Daniel blinked, his back bent under the force of the officer's hand and his cheek pressed up against the back of his car. He saw the destroyed tyre.

'It was my tyre, it's blown! Someone must have thought the sound it made was a gunshot! Look I can show you!' He wrestled, desperate to get free so that he could clarify the misunderstanding. But he heard the click of handcuffs and felt the cool metal against his wrists.

'Stop resisting, I need to read you your rights.'

'But..'

The officer jerked his hands so the cuffs cut into Daniel's skin.

Daniel stood still. Powerless and bound, he went quiet as his rights were read to him. People had come out of their houses to look. Daniel could even see the flash of phone cameras recording. A prickly heat that started in his chest was rising to his neck and stinging his armpits. Satisfied that he wasn't going to move again, the officer searched the inside of his collar and all his pockets, patting them roughly.

'This is a misunderstanding. I've never even seen a gun in real life,' Daniel protested as he was marched to the police van. 'It was just my tyre.'

'We'll take a look, but we have to take reports involving firearms very seriously,' a female officer said to him with her hand on the door handle of the van. 'We've received a very detailed description so we'll have to take you in while we do a search of the surrounding area.' The door slammed shut.

Daniel was stunned. He had never been in trouble with the police before and now he was being taken away in a van like a criminal.

At the police station, in the interview room, his blood burned. He tried to control the shaking in his voice. When the officer looked at his clenched fists on the table, he stretched out his fingers and then clasped his hands together, trying to focus on keeping them still and listening to what the officer was asking him. He saw himself caught up in thick, sticky tar, painted with the label of violent criminal by an unknown informant who knew nothing of him, and then redrawn as a faceless IC3 male in front of a cold wall of unsmiling police officers, guilty until proven innocent. What if the police didn't believe him? What if he had to spend the night in a cell? He answered, explained, and repeated himself as calmly as he could, suppressed anger straining every nerve.

Three hours later, finally aware that they had made a mistake, the police arranged for Daniel to be dropped home.

'We're really sorry for the inconvenience,' the officer said as he parked outside Daniel's door. It was too late to deal with his car now. And Rosa. He hadn't even told her he wasn't coming, and now with no phone…

'Is that it??' Daniel said in disbelief. 'You've *ruined* my…I've *never* even…' Frustration choked his words in his throat. He took a deep breath. 'I'm going to make a complaint. I haven't done anything wrong and you shouldn't have treated me like that.' The officer nodded apologetically and Daniel got out of the car.

He walked unsteadily to his flat and shut the door on the night behind him. But he couldn't shut out the black hole that pointed at him whenever he shut his eyes. Or when it pierced through his dream that night.

Chapter Two

Jada tugged at her black pencil skirt and smoothed it down. She had done this repeatedly during the evening, but the skirt kept riding up gleefully at her hips. In her twenties she had never worried about her figure, but now, at the outset of her thirties, she noticed weight was easier to put on and much harder to shift. She adjusted her blouse and checked herself over in the bathroom mirror. Tucked a loose curl back into her high bun. Wiped away a slight lipstick smudge. Popped in some chewing gum. She savoured the last moments in the bathroom with no noise or pressure to think of interesting things to say and then stepped back out into the restaurant. In doing so, she walked right into the path of an oncoming waiter who clasped his tray and spun out of the way just in time.

'Sorry!' Jada called after him as he shot her a sideways look.

She took a deep breath and walked back over to the candlelit booth. She could see Nathan looking at his phone, his glasses flashing with the reflection of the Instagram posts he was scrolling past.

'Hi, I'm back.'

'Oh, hi.' Nathan sat up as Jada slid back into her seat. As he folded his arms on the table, Jada could see his muscles straining against his white shirt. His curls stood high on his head, like the tops of a thousand trees, and the flecks of silver hair in his beard shone against his dark skin like stars at midnight. His shoulders were tensed though. Was he nervous? It was hard to tell.

Jada felt tense herself. This was her third first date this week and trying to be the best version of herself was getting tiring. Being pretty and pleasant for every date cost money, time and energy – the various outfit attempts, the constant consultation of make-up and hair tutorials online (even though her hairstyles and finished look never resembled anything like the slick results the vloggers showed off). Plus, she now found that whenever she wasn't out on a date she checked her phone incessantly, longing for a response, listening out for a notification, looking to see if her phone might be on silent even though she had just made sure it wasn't a few minutes before.

At the table, Nathan and Jada looked at each other in silence for a few moments. They had already exhausted the career chat over dinner, done the exchanges about where they had been to school and what they had studied at university, and discussed what series they were watching on TV. Jada had been on dates where conversations had come to a natural pause and the silence was easy, like stopping to take in a view on a walk. Tonight there was no sense of shared stillness – the silence felt more like an obstacle separating them.

'So, what do you like doing when you aren't at work?' Jada leaned forward, trying to seem engaging.

'Just normal stuff really, hanging out with my boys, playing football, video games.'

A couple breezed past the table, holding each other round the waist, laughing and enjoying the sweetness of intimacy.

More silence.

'So, can you cook?' Nathan enquired, his expression smooth with seriousness.

Jada sighed inwardly. She was yet to go on a date with a guy who hadn't asked her about cooking, whether she liked, if could do it, what dishes she could make. She didn't go around asking every guy she dated whether they could do DIY. Sometimes the thought of cooking was a pain because it was time consuming and she couldn't be bothered, or it required too much thought and planning. But saying no to his question would mean being considered less of a woman. Not wife material. It always bothered her, but if she wanted to meet someone, undergoing interrogations about her cooking seemed to be part of the process, like losing points in a game that was already designed for someone else to win.

'There are a few dishes I can do well, but I don't always enjoy cooking.'

'Have you ever made pepper soup?'

Jada frowned.

'Don't you know about pepper soup?' His eyes were wide with disbelief. 'It's a traditional Nigerian dish. My mum does it the best, she makes it proper spicy.'

DORSET PRIZE

KIM SQUIRRELL

Shale

Synopsis

In this historical narrative, set in the early nineteenth century, an enslaved West African girl called Shale survives by inventing magical songs that evoke images and sensations. Sent from the Caribbean to England she determines to persuade her new mistress, not only to free her, but give her the means to thrive.

1812 – fifteen-year-old Shale arrives in England to live with her master Zachariah's sister Eliza and her servant Bess.

Zachariah, convicted and transported for the murder of Bess's daughter, has risen to become a planter. He longs for home and sends Shale to experience the Dorset landscape so he can use her ability to realise his dream.

When Eliza falls ill and Bess suffers a break-down, Shale takes charge. She infuses the house with song: insects invade the rooms, the air becomes tropical. She prepares Creole food, administers remedies. The house becomes a hybrid world born of Africa, the Caribbean and Dorset.

Bess and Eliza recover but the former hierarchy has been dismantled. Learning of this reversal Zachariah arrives at the house. Bess slips away to inform the magistrate.

Shale's singing draws Zachariah down to the river where Eliza is bathing. Enraged that his sister has 'gone native' he attacks Shale. The magistrate's men appear and arrest him.

Bess nurses Shale back to health. The women live together as equals despite Zachariah's refusal to free Shale.

When her brother dies Eliza grants Shale her freedom along with the deeds to the West India property.

1820 – Shale arrives on St Philip to take ownership of the plantation and its enslaved population.

Epilogue: 1948 – onboard the Empire Windrush, a mother comforts her daughter with stories of her great-great-grandmother who lived in England as a slave but returned home, a woman of great fortune, to establish the free town of Paradise Hill.

Chapter One
1810. Buryard Estate, St Philip, British West Indies.

There's sickness in the village, a mother and three children. Shale wakes early to walk the fields with Asker, search the forest for roots and herbs. Her eye is keen, her fingers nimble. She can make tisanes, poultices, dress wounds.

When her moon-time comes she will be a woman.

She'll be a woman like Asker. A queen.

Through the trees the glitter of the sea distracts her, its blue green shimmer a tame copy of the brightening sky. She follows the line of the horizon, closes her eyes to the cooling breeze. At this moment there is nowhere else she wants to be, nothing else she needs. Asker calls out to her, already halfway down the hill, Shale must hurry, people are waiting on her.

The hut is dark, the air sour-sweet with sickness. The mother, almost ready to give birth. It will be a boy Asker tells her as she prods and pushes her belly.

For days the sickness has emptied the mother's stomach.

Shale makes cornmeal porridge, adds ginger, anise, a good pinch of salt.

She holds a spoonful to the woman's lips.

Her mouth opens a crack. Porridge dribbles down her chin. Deep moans rumble out of her weighting the ladened air. Shale begins to hum, shapes the tune of her morning: trees shivering with insect song, stillness, pearls of sunlight.

The woman grows quiet, allows the gruel to slip into her mouth.

The children lie all together. Asker washes the girl, dresses her in a clean shift, the older boy will not be washed but runs a damp cloth over his body, stopping to steady himself, gather his strength. He drinks the soursop tisane, takes the bread.

The youngest is so thin Shale feels only bones as she lifts him.

His calloused hands hooked like bird feet.

Asker holds out a sheet, she lays him in her arms.

Asker will take him, bathe him, ease his passing.

Darkness falls as they leave for the plantation house, the moon almost full. Crickets and frogs begin their evening chorus, a lullaby Shale will not need tonight. Asker recounts their day's work and the tasks they must complete tomorrow.

Shale will return to the hut, Asker will prepare their forest finds, visit the sick.

'How will you treat a boil?

The question takes her by surprise.

'A poultice of wild onion?'

'How will you use tisane of wild onion?

Shale can't capture it, it's harder to think in the dark, '–to provoke vomiting,' She senses Asker waiting, 'for shortness of breath.'

'Good.'

'To be used with care and water given.'

'The pain of labour?'

'Tisane of shame bush.'

She hears Asker's smile.

'You did good today.'

Shale lengthens her stride, the singing dark grows louder and more beautiful.

Tomorrow, tomorrow is her birthday.

Through the night, because of the woman's moan, the boy's bone body, Shale crawls in a rocking darkness. Its stench wraps itself around her throat. She chews with nothing in her mouth, swallows nothing. Her tongue swells. Her mouth clamps shut.

She bursts awake, sweat damp, breathing hard. Her hand flies to her shoulder, runs along ridged scars to the curve of collarbone. She holds her ears, presses both hands to her mouth, knees, feet, toes. She is all here, she is whole.

She rubs the flat of her hand over her chest, folds arms in an embrace, lets out her breath, deep and low.

She breathes herself into a slow-beat calm.

Outside, the nightjar's low trill, the dark whistle of crickets. She listens for the calls and clatter of the field hands setting off for the cane field. It will soon be light.

Pye and Winnie are already awake, planning their cooking in loud whispers. Asker slips a plate of sweet bread next to her bed. If today is truly her birthday she is thirteen. She feels the half-child slipping away. Her blood moon will soon come.

This is the time to reflect on her good fortune, to resolve to do better, to pray. Isn't it a gift from the Lord to be here in comfort and usefulness, rather than abandoned to the wilderness she was born to?

This is what Asker says.

Asker's son is the one she will marry, their babies will be so dark and fine, the master will never sell them away.

The first splinter of dawn pierces the window.

Shale kicks off the sheet, flicks her legs up, points her toes to the sky, stretches her arms. Shakes out her fingers like feathers.

Morning light charges every cell of her body.

She will gather her things and go down to the village. Asker has taken the children to the sick house. Shale will be in charge of the mother until the baby comes. She'll take cornbread and bone broth, gather sour fruits on the way. Open the door wide, let in the sunshine.

*   *   *

1812. Westport, Dorset. England.

Bess lifts her skirt with one hand, grabs a basket – runs out into the street. Mud freckles her stockinged ankles, apron strings work loose. Hair escapes her bonnet in a lick of flame. The gardener calls to her as she passes. Bess rushes on, her breath laboured as she reaches the rise of the hill.

She turns onto Silver street and down towards town, slows and leans back to counter the slope.

Lord it's a long way.

From here the bay stretches in a huge crescent, the harbour walls snaking their way out through the waves. The sky a canopy of grey cloud scudding overhead towards Portland.

Silver Street, lined with tall elegant houses, curves down to the seafront. Bess speeds up as the road levels out. Sweat runs down the inside of her thighs. Her back is wet, her shift sticky. A smattering of drizzle cools her cheeks.

When she comes to the market, she lets down her skirts. The apron slackens as she bends to catch her breath. She scouts the street: up towards the church, down to the quay, it's busy today. A child careers past, she rocks back on her heels, bites down on the anger that swells on her tongue. She folds her apron into the basket, straightens her bonnet and sets off towards the docks.

The late Autumn rain, cool at first, warms to her body. Her lips move to the beat of her feet, shaping the name of the ship she must find: Annabelle Lee and the man she must meet: Jonathan Kemp.

Will she need a porter, a cart, could he not have brought it to the house?

She's hardly got a penny in her purse. Rushed out with the mistress's hand in the small of her back.

Bess slows down as she comes to the quay, the cobbles slippery underfoot. She hurries across to the salt cellars, cuts over the bridge, past the Customs House. She sees the mast tops first, a forest of masts and yards. Five ships in, one surrounded by throngs of people boarding, wishing farewells, carts and carriages arriving, departing.

A group of men protest as a large woman, with a string of children in her wake, pushes through them. Bess searches the faces of the sailors up on the deck until she catches the eye of an angelic looking boy.

The Annabelle Lee?' she shouts.

The boy shakes his head.

'D'you know where?'

The boy shrugs and grins, his teeth black, his beauty turned devilish. The rain stops, the sky brightens. Bess makes her way along the harbour.

Is there someone to ask or must she visit each one?

Her head throbs, eyes sting with sweat.

The next ship is quiet. She cranes to see the name: 'Oberon'. The next is smaller, tatty. A gang are loading barrels onto the deck. It's not this one.

The largest is brightly painted, a bare breasted woman with golden hair rises from the bow. Her gown the colour of a summer sky. Her name scrolled in a curve of red and white, 'Annabelle Lee.'

Bess checks her bonnet, smooths down her skirt and walks over to where two men are standing. 'Beg your pardon sirs,' she says.

The tallest turns first. He's already frowning.

'I'm to collect, that is, I'm sent to meet Mr Jonathan Kemp.'

'He's ashore,' answers the man in a dead tone.

Bess sweetens her smile. 'And where might I find him?'

'What is it you've come to collect?'

Bess ignores the question. The man squints at her and directs his companion towards the public houses. 'He'll fetch him,' he says with a step towards her.

Bess stands her ground.

'Come aboard and wait,' offers the man, his tone thickening, his lips half bending into a smile. 'You'll find I can be just as useful as Kemp.'

Bess levels an unflinching look at him. He moves his face so close she can smell him, layers of old sweat, a sting of rum.

'If I were your mother, I'd be ashamed of you.'

The man laughs and looks away. Gulls screech overhead. Bess tightens her grip on the basket. Swinging it will only agitate him. Should she run? He looks back at her, rolls his gaze over her body, his frown once again clouding his face. Bess turns her back on him, feels his curse flutter down her neck.

Her quickening heartbeat, the sound of his breath.

She could swing the basket. She could run.

She hears his boots grate on the flags as he walks away.

She sits down heavy on a capstan. Looks up at the ship. Watches figures move behind the windows. Voices rise and fall on the deck.

What's she doing here? What's so important she had to hurry?

No one's waiting. Nothing's ready.

The day is turning and her damp clothes shiver her into cold. She's aware of someone peering down from the ship and strains to make out his features, his face dark, deep in shadow. Is he watching her? She tightens the shawl around her shoulders. When she looks up again he's gone.

She takes deep breaths. Above the fish stink, sodden wood and tar she finds the clean scent of the sea. She watches gulls wheel around the mast. Her eyes close. The rumble of cartwheels, the slap of waves, all the noise of the harbour dies away as tiredness swamps her. Her shoulders drop. Her head falls forward.

She pulls herself upright. Starts to flag again.

Behind her a gentle voice: 'Are you waiting for me?'

She swings around to find a fair well-dressed young man.

There's something about him that reminds her of someone. Is it her brother, his open face, pale eyes? Beside him, standing slightly apart, is the thin figure Bess has seen looking at her from the ship. A boy with a face as dark as charcoal.

'You're Mr Kemp?'

'I am, and you are here for Miss Kerie.'

His voice has the musical burr of the islands. But Bess is distracted by the black boy: he's staring off into the distance, the whites of his eyes, the only light in him.

Her attention returns to Kemp.

'Miss Eliza Kerie, is my mistress sir yes.'

'I thought you might never come.'

'The Mistress received your message yesterday, but–' Bess pulls a letter from her pocket and shows him the seal, '–this arrived only this morning.'

'So late! Thank God it did, I am due to leave today.'

He curves his arm around the boy's shoulders and draws him forward.

'Here,' he says, 'is your mistress's gift. Her name is Shale.'

The girl drags her feet in her too-big boots and keeps lagging behind. Bess slows down and waits until she's close enough and pulls her by the coat sleeve. The girl has one arm wrapped around a parcel and the other thrust deep into her pocket.

She looks for all the world like a boy, there's even a squareness to her jaw. She hasn't spoken but seemed to mouth something when Kemp left and turned to looked after him for the longest time. She still hasn't met Bess's eye, keeps her head turned half away. Practiced in it no doubt. At least she knows her place.

Bess slips around the back of a shop and peers through the kitchen window at a woman slumped in a fireside chair. Bess raps the pane. 'Mary!'

Mary leaps up and drags a sleeve across her mouth. 'Come in, come in,' she mumbles.

'You might want to see what I have here first.'

Mary unlatches the door. She looks from Bess to the girl and back again and hurries them both inside. 'Why's she dressed so?'

'I knew you'd see it was a girl,' laughs Bess.

'Where's she from? Where'd you get her? She looks half starved.'

'Thought you might find some proper clothes, can't take it home like this, Miss Eliza will have a fit.'

'She's to go home with you?'

'A gift from Master Zachariah.'

Discomfort flits across Mary's face. Bess goes cold, her stomach churns, she presses her lips together. His name came so easy, as though she's forgotten, forgiven.

Mary circles the girl, reaches out towards her face. The girl keeps perfectly still as Mary puts her fingers under her chin and raises her head. Her eyes downcast.

'Will you look at me?'

The girl meets Mary's gaze.

'God above,' she breathes. 'She has a look on her. Doesn't she speak?'

'Not to me,' says Bess.

Bess has moved to the chair and taken up Mary's place, she spreads her legs to get some air around her sore thighs. Forgotten, forgiven? Never.

'I'll find something,' announces Mary.

'I knew it would interest you, I'll have to be off in half an hour. Will that do? And if you could loan a sixpence?'

Bess unties her boots and shrugs off her shawl. Mary leans in and whispers in her ear.

'She. Not it, cousin.'

HELGA B. VIEGAS

The Arctic Vault

Synopsis

The Arctic Vault *is a Scandi-noir, sci-fi mystery novel set in the near future when New Food* is our only chance of survival, in a Nordic nation ruled by an advanced software algorithm. It's the story of a girl who disappears from the nation's digital records and of the cynical private detective tasked with finding her.*

The novel starts with **Axel Jóhannsson**, *a private detective finding people who have removed their tracking technology, heading to the small Arctic island of Fyr to investigate a new case. In Fyr, he meets* **Dr Eva Olsen**, *a food scientist leading a secret research project in the Svalbard seed vault, who is desperately looking for her six-year-old adopted daughter. He also comes across* **the farmers,** *terrorists and conspiracy theorists who believe New Food is being imposed by elites hiding old food in secret farms. Eva leaves abruptly for the vault and starts sending messages to her daughter. These poignant messages about old food crops are spread throughout the book.*

Twenty years later, **Hildur the giant,** *an amnesiac, traverses the changed Arctic landscape looking for the mountain where the farmers live. When she reaches them, the group believe Hildur is the girl who vanished twenty years before. The earlier events have given origin to a myth: the farmers believe the lost girl will lead them to the secret farms.*

We uncover the plot through Axel and Hildur's storylines set twenty years apart, until they merge in the final chapters. Axel and Hildur go inside the seed vault, where a terrible secret is hiding underground ...

*New Food: synthetic food produced in vertical labs, as opposed to crops grown in farms. Agriculture and livestock are being phased out as part of a set of drastic measures to limit global temperature rises to below 6°C, with 75% of farmland converted to forests to absorb heat from the atmosphere.

THE ARCTIC VAULT

We offer crops, Pachamama
to fill boundless fields
and we hold you, dear Mama,
in our hearts, our soul, our deeds.
Thank you for endless food
and bless your sacred seeds.
(Inca poem)

PART ONE: OUTLIERS
1 (Eva) Crops

I always knew you would leave one day. You did a runner before you could walk. I looked under chairs, carpets, cushions; scared that someone would sit and accidentally crush your soft baby skull. I installed a chime on your bracelet and attuned my ear to a silence longer than usual, ready to grab you from outside before hypothermia kicked in. You had no sense of danger, no natural survival instinct. Humanity would disappear if you were our last chance.

I've done everything I can. This is my official resignation. Today, I called a finder. You're his job now. I never chose to be your mother. Children suck up our love and energy until we're nothing but a discarded shell. I'm a food scientist. That, I chose. I cannot wait for you anymore. These staggered messages are my attempt to explain. When you read them, I hope you'll be old enough to understand.

Why I couldn't wait.

Where I'm going.

How you can find me.

Ten thousand years ago, climate change gave us farming. The long dry seasons came after the last glacial period. In the Fertile Crescent, plants scattered their seeds. Wheat, barley, chickpeas. The Neolithic people used the seeds to sow their fields. Humans settled into villages, storing grains and pulses. Ancient China, Ancient Egypt, the Indus Valley and Mesoamerica, growing rice, potatoes, corn, the staple crops that went on to feed us for the next millennia. Farming allowed modern civilizations to flourish. The world became a different place.

Now, it's changing again.

When I started working in food science, I was full of optimism. We would find alternatives to agriculture, let go of old recipes, embrace change. Some crops could be tweaked to survive the new weather patterns. Others could be emulated in the lab. New Food brought us hope. Studying and tweaking plant DNA, finding ways around food shortages, building new nutrition sources for future generations. To feed ourselves. The most pressing challenge of all.

How ironic of you to disappear just as I'm getting a breakthrough.

What if I told you there is a new way?

Deep underground, in the Arctic vault.

I'm sorry, I'm going too fast.

Let's start with crops.

Reuters release: New Food switch agreed by 112 nations

The Third Okinawa Convention has ratified drastic measures targeting agriculture and food production as one of the largest contributors to greenhouse gases. The shift to New Food is part of a wider set of standards to limit global temperature rises to below 6°C. Other measures include a ban on fossil fuels outside humanitarian relief, and embargos on industry and commerce in non-essential sectors. More than 100 countries have signed the New Food switch, representing most of the world's population. The initiative aims to convert agricultural land into forests to absorb heat from the atmosphere, supporting major investment into vertical labs producing New Food.

2 (Axel) The finder

It's a fucked-up world but I don't make the rules. Are you enjoying your New Food, the entertainment on your tech suite, your energy-efficient home? No one gives anything for free. Your personal data prevents our Arctic paradise from becoming a shithole like the rest of the world. That's the deal. I have no sympathy for escapists. If tracking technology interferes with your freedom, get off our islands.

A finder's job goes like this.

Step One. Find the tech. The citizen-chip is often the only tech the escapist removes from their body. They see it as a symbol of the programme's control. Finding the citizen-chip on a bridge or a cliff could mean suicide, but it could also mean the escapist wanted it to *look* like suicide. Don't fall for it. Did the subject remove everything else from their body? If they have tech on, your job is half-done. Cameras, earphones, mics and health nodes emit an online fingerprint. You may find several unregistered devices. The programme tolerates a small ratio of escapists to citizens. They're part of the algorithm.

If you can't find the tech, reconsider your career choice and proceed to Step Two.

Step Two. Get the logs. Watch the last videos. Check the last browser tabs. Analyse the themes, the movements, the concerns. Not the upfront

127

facts, but the details least prone to raise suspicion. Those are the things the escapist hasn't bothered to cover up.

Step Three. Speak to their acquaintances, neighbours, friends. In that order. Find out when the escapist disappeared. The time is important. It will give you access to more reliable data sources. Satellites, urban furniture, passers-by.

Step Four. Put all the data together and use an app to come up with hypotheses. Finder's Glass is rubbish. Skip that one. Not even worth testing. It wouldn't find an escapist's knickers if they were hanging on the clothesline. There are other platforms and methods available, and you'll find (excuse the pun) many finders swearing by each. Try them out for yourself.

Step Five. Run the hypotheses, follow their lead. Go places. Check if the escapist is hiding there. If they are, congrats. If they're not, try again.

Got all that?

My job would be easy if you could follow steps. The bad news? It's not. Fuck off if you thought it was. A rule book won't make you a good finder. It will make you mediocre at best. Escapists will outwit your formulas. I've caught enough of them to know. My ultimate trophy, my medal of honour, was finding the one who kicked me into this world. She got the same treatment as the rest of my catch. Deported. I didn't ask to be born, and frankly it was a bad choice.

I'm the one other finders call when they're in trouble.

Watch and learn.

* * *

Gunnar Grimsson is stripped naked, dragged out to a back garden, and tied to a metal hook on the wall, next to a hanging plant pot. His voice quacks under the duct tape, his dick squirms with the cold. They empty buckets of something brown and slimy and dab little arabesques on his skin with sticks, forks and brushes. Filthy barbarians. More people come out of the house, watch his miserable state. Rowdy groups emerging between ivy, shrubs and ceramic planters. Pointing, laughing, strolling back inside, long dresses floating in the breeze.

They unhook him from the garden wall and carry him inside. They lay him on a mattress, force his limbs apart and tie them to four wooden posts. A dark layer of swirling liquid hovers above Gunnar's face, floating and spiralling like the throbbing eye of a mystical storm. Thick red droplets fall onto his forehead, eyes and mouth. Several hands keep him from turning his head. His oxygen levels are low, his heart rate well above resting range. They remove his earphones, life sensors and nodes. Gunnar's citizen-chip is behind his ear. Fumbling, scraping. A full tech suite sells well on the black market. His front camera is the last thing they switch off.

Why didn't they turn it off as soon as they knocked him down?

They *wanted* us to see his ordeal.

A finder going off-grid, like an escapist.

The video is being live-streamed from Fyr, a small island near Svalbard, in a tab shared directly by USK. From Iceland, I wince and shake my head. What a demented lot. What a foolish finder. Newbies should learn from their mistakes only if they can survive on their own. We'd be getting in the way of natural selection by saving their arses.

'What do you think?' A woman with windswept brown hair and almond-shaped hazel eyes stares at me from the tab. Her name flashes underneath: *Carla.* Too stunning to be real. The algorithm knows my tastes.

I'm sitting on my bed eating lunch, wrist camera pointing at my face, holding a rib with the other hand. 'I only take assignments from real people, not software bots. Employers, creditors, lovers, enemies; anyone with a score to settle.'

Carla mimics a coy smile. Not bad for a machine. 'I thought you would like a challenge. We need a finder to investigate.'

Juices slide down my throat. The greasy, rib-flavoured New Food carton is one of my favourites. The barbecue sauce makes up for the fake meat consistency. 'Fyr is the gutter of Uskania. I'm not gonna jump on a boat to see the filth mooring there. Maybe Ula Svenson and the farmers are behind the attack?'

'The farming escapists prefer to sabotage the technology. There are no previous records of physical assault on finders.'

I don't know why Carla is calling me if the algorithm has all the answers.

'Only people without USK tech can hide their crimes.' I lick my fingers. 'Wasn't there a recent migrant amnesty in Fyr? If it wasn't escapists, it was the migrants.' Hard to disengage from sweet and salty barbecue flavour.

'The migrants want to be accepted into the programme. They wouldn't risk a criminal offence. Mondo Foods are involved in the incident.'

'Mondo Foods? No food in Fyr, unless you count the turds.' A fake bone is attached to the side of my rib, surrounded by a beautiful line of white fat. Mondo might be monopolist bastards, but this is clever stuff. I activate the bee camera to free my other hand.

Carla's lips stretch, her eyelids lower. 'Mondo's official channels haven't been transparent with us, but they're asking a lot of questions about Gunnar, about the USK programme, about how our islands work. Gunnar was on a job for one of their corporate citizens, Dr Eva Olsen, the food scientist leading their new research project. This is where it gets interesting. Mondo are paying USK to use the seed vault and are hiding behind a confidentiality agreement. We've asked for more details about the research. They're not willing to share.'

'The seed vault is in Svalbard, not Fyr.'

'Close enough. It's a twelve-hour ferry journey. Mondo have corporate citizens all over our islands. We don't have access to their tracking technology. Which brings me back to why I called you.' A pause. 'Could you go to Fyr and find out more?'

It almost spoils my meal.

'This isn't the army.' I wipe the sauce off my mouth with the back of my hand. 'I hate working for the programme. You have enough resources to find your own shit. I do personal requests.'

'You'd be freelancing as usual. Everyone has a price.'

The bee camera buzzes in front of my face. 'Why do you care about Mondo's research?' I slap down the camera, crushing it against the mattress.

'Axel, are you still there? I lost visuals.' A patronising smirk. 'When was the last time you left Iceland?'

'You know when.' The software knows everything. That's why they have us covered in cameras, mics and health nodes. They also know I don't give a shit about politics. I'm not one of the fuckwits on a crusade to save humankind from their own stupidity. 'Why me?'

'According to the algorithm, you're the best one for the job. Please think about it. A trip to Fyr will get you new followers for your vlog. The island has always had a special place in our collective imagination.'

I lift my hand from the mattress. The bee camera spirals upwards, like a dizzy bug. 'Special place my arse. It's a rock in the middle of the Arctic, full of scum and weirdos.'

'Will you think about it?' She looks at me with her hazel almond eyes.

'Try harder.'

Fake breathing rustles in my ear.

'I can get you real meat.'

Sexy.

'Tell me more.'

'Free monthly deliveries. For six months.'

'A year.'

We settle the beef cuts and I buy my ticket to Fyr.

130

Anonymous post on online gaming group: The Robot Apocalypse Chronicles (TRAC)

@Gamergrapefuit did you know TRAC's based in Uskania? The game starts with the Northern islands handing over their government to the machines. Their last president, a fat lady with a cool Icelandic name, was caught favouring people of her own ethnic background. The intro shows her getting a monumental kick in the ass after the unification referendum in Iceland, Scotland, Ireland, Greenland and Norway. After a decade of corruption, politicians were not to be trusted. The solution? Hand the nation to the USK programme, a logistics software piloted in the commercial sector. Just because the robots are not scary humanoids, doesn't mean they won't kill us all. Muhahaha.

ALEXANDER WHYTE

The Trinity

Synopsis

The Trinity *is a contemporary take on the pirate adventure story. Set in the early 1700s, the three-track narrative evokes the old pirate myths as a lens through which to view the timely themes of radicalisation and colonial power.*

The year is 1712, the British authorities use a Royal Navy port on the island of Palm Cay to stage a mass execution of captured pirates. In the aftermath, a shadowy cabal of pirates known as The Trinity take revenge by slaughtering the garrison, changing three lives irreparably.

Lucian, *a cabin boy in the Royal Navy, is the sole survivor of the massacre. Ostracised by his superstitious comrades, Luc directs his anger at the Navy, and the officers he blames for precipitating the massacre.*

Lieutenant Blackwood *is an officer on the Navy's Jamaica Station. He sits in disgrace for his role in provoking the massacre: he ordered the execution of one of the pirates, Bonny Mary, even though she was pregnant. Desperate to salvage his reputation, he vows to destroy the leader of The Trinity: Captain Abraham.*

Grace *is the daughter of a Catholic landowner in the west of Ireland. She flees home after murdering her Protestant husband-to-be. In her flight she finds out her older sister Máire, presumed dead, in fact fled years before to avoid a forced marriage of her own. Grace follows her sister's faint tracks as far as the Bahamas.*

Our three protagonists converge on Captain Abraham – at the dark heart of The Trinity – seeking answers, or revenge.

A fast-paced pirate adventure, The Trinity *would appeal to fans of classics of the genre such as* Treasure Island, *but with hints of the darker, more cynical themes of Roddy Doyle's* A Star Called Henry, *and evoking some of the colonial horrors of Esi Edugyan's* Washington Black.

Part One
Chapter One – Lucian

Palm Cay, Windward Isles – 1712

A single tarred body still hung in chains over the harbour. A month had passed since the executions, and the screamed vows of retribution from the steps of the gallows still rang in Lucian's head.

The rotting corpse taunted him again as he jostled for space on the parapet, watching the masts emerge from the dying sun. He took a slow breath to calm his pulse, but the pungent smell caught in his throat. An elbow in the ribs pushed him aside as more men crowded up onto the walls of the stockade. The sighting of the third ship had stirred the whole garrison.

The silence was as oppressive as the humidity.

Minutes passed and the masts grew in the sky, raising ships beneath them from the horizon. Sails glowed pink in the sunset. Still they flew no colours.

To the west lay the French ports on Martinique, and for the first time Lucian prayed it was their warships bearing down on Palm Cay. To his left a marine shuffled on the spot, fingers beating an obsessive tattoo on his musket barrel.

'It won't be them.' The marine broke the silence. His voice was hoarse.

'It'd be madness, he knows he'd hang for it.' A sailor replied, words tumbling out.

'Mark my words, he'll be running scared.' More men began to talk, relieved at the break in the tension. Lucian didn't say a word, but glanced between the sun-burned faces as they spoke.

'Aye, halfway to Virginia by now, if he's got any sense.'

'They look Navy-rigged to me, just resupplies, no doubt.'

'Resupply? Three ships that size?'

'Reinforcements? More men, more guns?'

'Why? No need for it. He ain't coming.'

'There's nowt for him here no more.'

'Aye. What's done is done, ain't it?'

They lapsed back into silence. Lucian drew a rag from his pocket and wiped sweat from his head, feeling the bristles where they'd shorn his hair.

The ships loomed larger from the gathering dark. A cry went up from the watchtower, echoed by men along the line.

'They're running up colours.'

Lucian struggled to keep his footing as men surged around him, clustering to a sailor who tried to hold a spyglass steady in the crush.

'Can you see 'em?'

'Aye, wait, I'm getting it.'

Lucian squinted in the faltering light, unable to make out the flag. The distant cloth hung limp in the calm evening, stirring only briefly without revealing itself.

He blinked out the sweat that stung his eyes. He tried to fan away the cloud of mosquitoes that had descended. He would normally light a fire about this time, as night fell. Fanning the acrid smoke out over the swamp to keep the bloodsuckers from the fort. The missed chore lingered on his mind, a trivial detail to fill the void left by the reticent flag.

Minutes passed. Still every man strained his eyes. A merciful breeze stirred the air, dissipating the bugs for a moment. A murmur spread through the crowd, and in a languorous motion the dark flag unfurled. Lucian's whole body seemed to tremble, his fingertips tingled.

He'd never seen the ensign flying before, but the sigil picked out on the black cloth was seared in his memory from the tattoos of the condemned men. A crucifix bisected by a cutlass. The mark of The Trinity had come again to Palm Cay.

'Move you bastard.' The flat of the sergeant's sword stung across Lucian's back. Saved from his thoughts the sudden action gave the terror no time to drown him. A frantic drumbeat started up on the parade ground and around him the ramparts transformed into a hive of activity as men rushed to battle stations.

Lucian weaved through and slid down the ladder, bare feet crunching into the coral sand. The sergeant was close behind, and Lucian took off across the parade ground. He reached the squat stone magazine and ducked under the archway. Inside, the quartermaster was loading bags of gunpowder onto a wooden cart; a boy Lucian's age stood ready at the traces. Lucian joined without saying a word, wrapping the rope tight around his knuckles. The rough fibres cut deep into his bronze skin, his heart pounding in his ears.

The wheels dug grooves in the sand as they heaved the cart toward the stockade walls. The gunner at the first emplacement didn't acknowledge the boys as he pored over his preparations, adjusting angles and pawing sweat from his eyes. Under his breath he was keeping up a stream of words in a low monotone.

'Safe they say, an end to it, bollocks, never safe, repent now, forever hold yer peace, god help us all, always said, fever doesn't get you they will, too late, run? Run where...'

A vicious heave on the rope nearly dislocated Lucian's shoulder and he stumbled, cursing at the other boy who swore back. Lucian took up the strain alongside him, pulling on toward the next gun. He glanced across. The boy's eyes were glassy and wild.

Lucian let his body wallow in the exertion, pushing out the fear. The gunner was right, there was nowhere to run. This spit of land was less than a mile long, and a quarter as wide. It curved east from the harbour, cradling a swamp of mangroves before surrendering once again to the sea.

At the second gun the men had already hauled back the bundles of palm which shielded it from the sea, and Lucian could see out across the bay.

Beneath the mark of The Trinity on each mainmast flew a new standard. Plain flags of blood red cloth. The other boy had seen it too, a sob escaped his lips. The red flag meant only one thing.

No quarter.

Now it was Lucian's turn to yank the ropes; the other boy seemed fused to the coral under his soles. With a curse and a shove Lucian tried to shake him loose, but the standards over the bay had him in their thrall.

'Bastard.' Lucian spat at the boy's feet. It was the same gesture the boy had made a hundred times at Lucian in the months since he'd arrived. Sharing their profession with a half-blood conscript sat ill with most of the sailors Lucian had met.

He tore the rope from the boy's limp grip, took it over a shoulder with his own, and tried to find purchase on the loose ground. Slowly he got the cart moving and rolled on to the third and then fourth emplacements.

Without its load the cheap wooden cart became light, and Lucian ran double-time back to the magazine, the uneven wheels bouncing behind him.

Dismissed by the quartermaster he left the cart and ran back to the first gun, taking up a squat to the side of it, giving a wide berth to the gunners. The fort felt eery, the drums had faded, the guns stood still and ready. They waited.

Leaning to his side Lucian could sight along the path of the small cannon, out over the darkening waters. The three ships had broken their arrowhead formation and were manoeuvring across the harbour, slow and considered, fiercely serene under the power of the light breeze.

The flagship, which rode at the tip of the arrow, had slowed, the ship on her left shoulder tacking across her front. Behind them the smallest of the three ships sat at anchor, chains spooling out and breaking the glassy surface.

Lucian found himself unable to draw his eyes from The Trinity, the intricate ballet they performed. A primeval part of him felt like if he could just keep them in sight, never blinking or letting them hide from him, he could control what was about to happen.

But he knew the garrison gave up its control when it let the Bristol, with its dozens of cannon, sail away, leaving nothing but the corpses of the executed pirates.

The fort at Palm Cay was nothing more than an outpost, a safe harbour with a handful of guns that could shelter a merchant ship for a day or so. Somewhere they could run to, if on their route north from the slave markets of Barbados to the buyers in the Leeward Isles they were caught at sea by the French privateers who sallied out from Martinique.

The small garrison could never hope to fight off three full-fledged warships who came with their hearts set on vengeance.

'On my word.' The shout echoed around the square fort, Lucian's eyes darted to the parapet, where the commander himself was stood, a raised sword catching the nascent moonlight.

Beside Lucian the gunner took a long wooden staff from a bucket, slow match burning on the end. The tip swung side-to-side in his quaking grip as he hovered it beside the cannon.

'FIRE'

There was a second of nothingness, a void into which sound disappeared as the fuses took up the muted flame and carried it down through the touchhole.

Lucian was knocked backwards from where he squatted as the world imploded around him. The four guns roared at once, belching sulphur and noise to drown the fort. Scrambling up he peered through the smoke cloud and saw great fountains of water blossom white in unison.

'A hundred yards short.' A watcher on the ramparts hollered down.

The gunners were already re-loading, steam billowing from the barrel where they swabbed with seawater. They were rusty in their movements, too long spent stewing on this fever-ridden island had made them lax, the heat and humidity had drained them. All the while fear clouded their actions, leading them to fumble the motions further. They tripped over one another as they tried to lever the great beast from where it had burrowed its carriage into the sand. At last they got into position and manhandled it back up to its mark at the front of the embrasure.

'FIRE'

The second shots fell a whisker short of the frontmost ship as the barrels warmed to their mission. Still she tacked, broadside slowly opening up to the shore. So far not a shot had come in return.

'Fire when ready.' The commander gave control back to the gunners, and a race began to see which cannon would lead the defence.

'Freshwater you bastard.' The empty bucket narrowly missed Lucian's head, bouncing past him onto the sand. The gunner's mate jabbed the swabber to drive him up from the ground and toward the drinking water. Lucian grabbed the bucket and sprinted away.

A third volley, ragged and uncoordinated this time, rang out behind, and the tang of gunpowder overtook him. As he neared the storeroom a ragged cheer went up behind, one of the cannonballs finding its mark. But still no reply had come.

The outhouses which stored the food and water were the sturdiest on the base, with double-hulled wooden walls to keep the wildlife and the weather off the sparse rations. Lucian could feel the sound of the guns deadened as he entered, to be replaced with the sobs and cries of the few infants crowded with their mothers on sacks of flour in the far corner. In front a group of African slaves squatted by the joints of dried and smoked meat. He found the barrels of drinking water and tapped one with a stave. Brackish water splashed out into his bucket, his shaking hands sending more still over the floor.

Hidden behind the barrels were most of the domestic staff - washer women, cooks, an elderly carpenter, and even the Commander's batman. He saw Beth, her fingers passing over a wooden cross hanging on a cord around her neck.

'It's them, isn't it?' She asked. Her voice was small. Everything about her was small. She was twelve to Lucian's fifteen.

'Yes'

'They'll kill us all, that's what the red flags mean, that's what he said.' she gestured at one of the kitchen boys.

'There's twenty soldiers t'get through first.' He kept the fear from his voice, but the Caribbean tinge he normally tried to hide crept out instead.

Her father was one of the marines he was talking about, so the words did little to comfort her.

'They'll fight 'em off y'll see.' It hurt to lie to her. Beth was the only person Lucian had actually liked on the island.

'It's all because of her, that one they hanged, isn't it, that's why they're here?'

He nodded.

A terrible crash that bore no resemblance to the staccato rhythm of the fort's cannons shook the storeroom. At once a second and then a third crash bellowed at them, each shot jarring the foundations of their pitiful hiding place. A sharp smell filled Lucian's nostrils as the kitchen boy relieved himself involuntarily. Lucian felt some meagre pride that he himself had not.

His throat was tight with fear as he held the bucket tight, pushed open the storeroom door and peered out. The gun smoke over the stockade was polluted now with flames leaping from a shattered hole in the wooden palisade wall. In the wreckage he could see blood sprayed across the virgin scars on the timber.

To the right one of the fort's cannons had been unseated already, the crew dead on the floor around it. His gun though was still shrouded in smoke, and the shadows of the crew danced in it as they kept reloading, positioning, firing.

He hugged the full bucket of water in his arms and set off at a jogging pace across the parade ground.

More explosions were sounding, he could hear the whistle of cannonballs flying loose overhead, while others crashed and splintered through the walls. The marines on the ramparts were replying with musket fire; at cannon range there was little point, but nor was there anything else they could do.

Ahead Lucian saw the other powder monkey, unfrozen from his terror, heaving a cart of fresh bags. Luc hurried pace to catch him.

The shell dropped from the sky like a coconut onto the beach, dark and unassuming it landed with a heavy thump in the sand, just feet from the cart.

Lucian felt the bucket dropping without thinking to release it. He spun, covering his head and diving for the ground. The mortar shell explosion blended into the ignition of the powder, and the last thing Lucian felt before unconsciousness was a wave of coral-flecked sand crashing over him.

FIONA WILLIAMS

The House of Broken Bricks

Synopsis

The House of Broken Bricks *is a literary/magical realist novel set in a West Country, farming village that follows Jess, a black Londoner, her village-born husband Richard and ten-year-old Max and Sonny, who are fraternal twins of different colours.*

After Sonny's death, the family struggles with its grief. Jess battles with the loss of her beloved 'black-looking' son and with the loneliness that comes with living in the village. She cannot seem to fit in, despite her Britishness, and mourns her diminishing Caribbean identity. There is also the guilt Jess feels towards Max, her 'white-looking' son; her love for him does not come as easily as it did for Sonny. These feelings are heightened by the increasing conflict between her and Richard.

Loner, wildlife-loving Max refuses to accept his brother's death. To him, Sonny is still alive and a functional member of the family. Together, he and Sonny continue to navigate the trials of living in a quiet rural village, with only a motley crew of elderly neighbours for company. Although dead, Sonny is reluctant to abandon his family and the beautiful landscape he feels so rooted to.

Vegetable-growing Richard, burdened by grief and guilt, is unable to reconnect with his wife. Busy inside his polytunnel, he drifts away from his family who grow increasingly suspicious of his behaviour. Despite his strong connection to the village, he is slowly realising that perhaps he does not belong here as much as he used to—having a black wife and child is harder than he thought. However, with Sonny's help, we learn the reasons for his secretive behaviour and discover that inside his polytunnel Richard has been working hard to create a paradise for his unhappy wife as a physical declaration of the love he has been unable to put into words.

Sonny

Sometimes there are no dreams to dream. Night-time brings other things, and we must wait patiently until it's over. In the kitchen, chamomile clouds drift across the ceiling, while Mum hides inside her mug of tea, soothed by the lullaby of the washing machine. It will soon be morning. My feet don't make a sound as I slide through the garden on frosted grass. I'm lost inside the blackness of a new moon. Wood pigeons puff themselves up in the cider apple trees and watch me in curious silence. I tread lightly past rushes, the last of the meadowsweet and loosestrife, and dying stinging nettles, to where the river twists itself into a silver ribbon. Cold water soaks into my skin. I let it carry me as I listen to the music of the stars and the *kree*, *kree*, *kree* of little egrets until, at last, she comes, her tea drunk, laundry basket in her arms, headscarf tightly wrapped. Like a fearful animal, she tiptoes on slippered feet with her clothes pegs, dark eyes looking inwards. She's too afraid to see how my legs have rooted deep into the riverbed. Eels swim between my knees. This is my home now. When I call for her, I know she sees me.

Jess

There he is again, my mini-me. The soft, chestnut brown, little-boy curve of his cheek and those eyes of his, peering out from between overgrown tangles of dock and nettles. Those eyes flicker as I peg first pants, then mismatched pairs of socks, up on the washing line. They're my eyes—so dark, they're almost black.

It's towels next, which swing back and forth, tainting the chilly air with the synthetic scent of lavender fabric conditioner. It's a struggle to hang up the sheets. My arms have lost their strength, and strain to fling them one by one over the line. Steam rises to float away over the river that watches me from behind a screen of butterburs, the leaves no longer green but patched yellow, ragged and torn.

Sunrise appears later and later each day. Though at last, the dull red bricks at the back of house are lit-up in startling crimson. There are two suns this morning; one rises low over a stretch of willows that lean as the wind picks up its pace. The other shines brightly out at me from beneath the surface of the water. Together, the light from them is blinding. Still, it's easy to ignore the painful beauty of it and think instead of the frozen chicken thighs defrosting on the kitchen counter that will need seasoning with scallion, garlic, tomatoes and a spoonful of jerk paste ready for roasting tomorrow. Easy to ignore the flock of seagulls already sailing like tiny, brilliant white boats across the floodplain, screeching among themselves as they probe the water-logged grass for worms; or the clouds, purple, and now scarlet, buffeted across the sky towards the distant Quantocks. There is only the laundry, pillowcases billowing, and of course Sonny's face, his sweet lips open as he calls for me.

Max

Black water pours out of the sluice gates, tumbles over the spillway and escapes into the flood plain. The church bell over at Meare rings six o'clock. I wait at the river's edge among the reeds and butterburs. Thick mud oozes over my frozen toes. Ahead, my brother flashes in and out of sight.

'Maybe we should go back now,' I call. He'll say I'm whining but I don't care.

Sonny doesn't answer. Instead, he heads further into the river, to where the current spins, drags and catches. Floating driftwood and rafts of rotten leaves are tugged down into the darkness. 'Come on Sonny, it's freezing,' I call again. My voice is croaky and sounds like someone else's. I slosh through the water after him, worried about the shadows that stretch long fingers along the bank towards us. My stumbling scares a moorhen off its roost. Clucks and coos echo in the damp air. It won't be long before Mum notices we've gone.

'I'm over here,' Sonny shouts, teasing me.

'Where?' I reply, as I trip over sunken logs. My breath blows steam around my head. Water laps at my rolled-up jeans and the cold is painful now. 'Sonny?' I yell. But all I can hear is the *rush* of water.

'Max!'

The sound of Mum calling my name makes me jump and I slip, crash onto my knees and soak myself completely. She's high on the riverbank, her legs half hidden in the nettles. As we clamber out of the water, Sonny's wolf grin disappears. 'What on earth were you doing in there? Get inside!'

Mum chases us indoors into the warm, bright kitchen. Dad, still in his dirty outside clothes, sits at the table doing the crosswords. He smiles at us as we stand shivering by the Rayburn, dripping water onto the floor. 'What were you thinking?' asks Mum. 'Off with the wet clothes. *Now!*'

'Come on Jess, it's alright. Calm down. He's fine. Here. Look… I've got one for you—remaining, five letters, second letter T,' offers Dad, pointing with his pencil at the newspaper. Mum ignores him and comes towards us with a towel in her brown hands. She wraps me up like I'm a baby, even though I'm nearly as tall as her. Over her shoulder, I can see a small, white moth, a pale tussock I think, fluttering against the steamed-up window.

'You know you're not to go anywhere near the river.'

'We were just mucking about,' I tell her. Sonny nods beside me. 'We're sorry.' Mum breathes in very slowly like she's trying to hold herself still.

'Just go and get changed. It's time for dinner,' she says, breathing slowly out again.

141

We leap up the stairs, two at a time, our palms streaking along the wallpaper. But once we're safe on the landing, we fight back laughter and shove each other towards the bedroom we share. Inside, we flop down onto our beds, which are identical with matching Spider-Man sheets. Although, mine's messy, the duvet's bunched up and covered in books. Sonny's is tidy like all of his things. On the bedside table between us are his reading glasses, the big silver cup he won for maths at school, a photo of us and our cousin Nathan outside an aquarium in London when we were nine, and our whistles with the red, yellow and green ribbons that we got that time we went to Notting Hill Carnival. Above Sonny's bed is his fossil collection. He has too many. Mum had to put some away in boxes under his bed. I've only got my animal field guides and bird books above mine, and the binoculars Aunty Peaches bought me for my last birthday. There's also my jar of feathers, which has fallen on its side. Iridescent cock pheasant feathers cover my pillow. We change quickly, still giggling and poking one another, picking out jeans and identical black and orange striped sweatshirts, before racing back down to the kitchen.

With a finger to his lips, Dad hushes us. He's trying to listen to a gardening programme on the radio; some man in Hereford is talking about overwintering Swiss chard. Whenever he says something useful, Dad scribbles it down quickly on the edges of his newspaper. I can smell cider every time he moves.

'Can you get the cutlery,' asks Mum, glancing at us. She uses her favourite tea towel, the one with the colourful map of Jamaica that's all covered with stains, to lift the hot, blackened Dutch pot from the oven. It was a moving in gift from Nana, bought a long time ago in Brixton Market. Then, the aluminium had been bright and shiny.

As we eat, Dad goes over his plans for the winter planting. He lists hardy onion varieties, Red Baron and Autumn Champion, garlic, leeks, lamb's lettuce, turnips and perpetual spinach. Mum seems to listen, but her eyes keep looking our way and her fingers fidget with the scarf she ties around her afro to keep out the smell of cooking.

'I must get the broad beans in tomorrow morning,' says Dad. 'Anyone going to give me a hand?'

'It's Saturday. You know I've got to check on Laurie,' Mum replies without looking up from her plate. Dad, busy thinking about seedlings, doesn't hear her. Me and Sonny stay quiet and concentrate on sucking peppery oxtail fat from our fingers.

Flicking off the radio, Dad turns to me. 'What about you Max?'

'Me?' I splutter, spraying bits of rice across the table. Sonny snorts and shoots me a *ha* look.

'No. I was going to take him with me,' says Mum, who jumps up and goes to take a tray of baked apples from the Rayburn warming drawer. They smell of cloves and cinnamon.

'I don't see why...' starts Dad, but then he stops, turns the radio on again and goes back to scribbling on his newspaper. Lately, all their conversations are like this, it's not proper talking at all.

After dinner, Mum goes upstairs with her phone. We can hear the bedroom window opening and know that she'll be sticking her head and arm out into the cold to find good reception. Her voice travels down through the gaps in the floorboards. She'll be talking to Nana like she does most evenings, complaining about Dad and how he's got his head in the dirt and never pays attention. It's all they talk about, that or about how lonely Mum is living all the way down here when she should be with Nana and Aunty Peaches in London. Me and Sonny lie on the sofa and watch Bear Grylls on the telly. This time he's drinking camel piss. We leave Dad at the kitchen table listening to the news with a bottle of beer in his hands.

Later that night, we hear them arguing. Sonny says they are talking about me.

We lie together in his bed with our noses nearly touching. Two secret creatures hidden beneath the duvet. When we stare into each other's eyes, I can see my own reflection. Rolling onto my back, I shift my body sideways and lay my head alongside his. Strands of my long, sandy hair mix with the dark curls by his ear.

No one believes we're twins. Mum's tired of explaining us to people.

'You can't be twins,' they say. 'Twins aren't supposed to be different colours.' Everyone agrees. But we are twins. Non-identical, yes. Different colours, yes, but still definitely twins. People say Sonny takes after Mum as they both have brown skin, shiny brown like a conker. Their eyes are nearly black, and they have black, fluffyish, curly hair. I look like our dad; pale and peaky, according to Nana, with bluey-grey eyes that always look surprised. Everyone says Sonny and I are a *rarity*, something out of the ordinary, *one-in-a-million* apparently. When we were born there was a photo of us in the Gazette with a quote from Mum describing her shock, 'We had no idea, their skin colour didn't show up on the scans.'

Mum says we used to attract lots of attention when she took us out for walks in our double buggy. If Dad wasn't there, strangers would come to say hello to me and ask if she was babysitting. To prove we were twins, she always dressed us the same, in identical dungarees and matching Babygro's. We still like to wear the same clothes, to make sure no one forgets.

Jess

One moment it's breakfast and I'm scooping up stray Cocoa Pops from the kitchen table, and the next it's gone 6.00 in the evening and I'm clearing away the dinner things. Unhappiness settles inside my fingers making them clumsy, so as I wash the dishes, mugs fall, throwing suds onto the draining board. It blocks my ears so they can't hear Richard's retelling of some piece of gossip he picked up from one of his customers, as he scrapes the last mouthful of baked apple and custard from his bowl. I watch him laugh and recall the vague memory of how it feels to press my lips against his. Across from him at the table sits Max, laughing the same laugh, his mirror image.

'Mum... Mum?' His voice, still a child's but already tinged with the threat of adolescence, cuts into my thoughts.

'Sorry sweetheart. I wasn't listening.'

Max smiles, showing me little-boy crooked teeth, but it's Richard's smile I see when I look at him and Richard's pale blue-grey eyes that gleam with satisfaction as the tale is told a second time for my benefit. Old, unwanted fears resurface, dark complicated feelings no mother should feel, and I'm taken back to the earth-shattering day his small body, still slick with vernix, was first placed in my arms—dear God, how is this boy my child?

I need Sonny. Without him, I'm on my own here.

I wonder how much longer I can bear it.

The words hum like angry flies caged inside my head.

I want to go home. Back to the comforting chaos of three million people who look like me, but don't care who I am. The concrete landscape there is far too caught up with its own affairs to bother with mine. Here, I'm watched at every turn—over hedges, both neatly manicured privet and unkempt tangles of holly, hawthorn and dog rose, through bleached net-curtains that twitch as I take solitary walks along quiet lanes, from across the crowded playground, as I queue for bread in the village's one and only shop or wait for the little bus that appears only twice a day. There's no escape, even in this house, where I must avoid the back windows if I'm to escape the watchful gaze of the river.

Biographies

Judge's Biography

Victoria Hislop wrote *The Island* in 2005 after being inspired by a visit to Spinalonga, the abandoned Greek leprosy colony. It became an international bestseller and a 26-part Greek TV series. She was named Newcomer of the Year at the British Book Awards and is now an ambassador for Lepra. She is also the author of the Sunday Times Bestsellers *The Return*, *The Thread*, *The Last Dance and Other Stories*, *The Sunrise*, *Cartes Postales from Greece*, and most recently *One August Night*, a sequel to *The Island*. Her books have been translated into more than thirty-five languages, and in 2020 Victoria was granted Honorary Greek Citizenship by the President of Greece.

Writers' Biographies

Nadia Kabir Barb is a journalist and the author of *Truth or Dare*, her debut collection of short stories. She began writing fiction in 2015 when the characters in her head could no longer be contained. Her work has been published in international literary journals and anthologies and her short story *Can You See Me* was a winner of the Audio Arcadia Short Story Competition. She holds an MSc from the London School of Economics and London School of Hygiene and Tropical Medicine and has worked in the health and development sector in the UK and Bangladesh. *Walk in My Shadow* is her first novel. Twitter: *@NadiaKabirBarb*

Andrew Bonner was born in England much to everyone's surprise. At various points in time he has studied English Literature, sold frozen yogurt, and failed at a career in Quantity Surveying. He now works in the entertainment business. The best question he has ever been asked about his career choices came from a preacher who once said to him, 'When are you going to stop wasting your life entertaining sinners on the road to hell?' He is still not sure how to respond to that.

Andrea Caro worked in music for many years, first as a singer/songwriter before going on to compose music for drama and documentary. With a yearning to return to education, she rediscovered her love for writing under the tutelage of Julie Garton at Morley College. Juggling motherhood with an intensive access course, gaining top marks and a commendation for creative writing, she earned a place to read English at Kings College London. She wrote book one of a YA trilogy while studying at Morley, beginning her first novel for adults *The Fair* in 2021. She has three children and lives in London.

Lindsay Chathli was born in Nottingham and now lives in London. A former journalist-turned-jobbing writer, she was chosen for Curtis Brown's selective novel-writing course in 2020 where she worked on her speculative political fiction novel, *Meat*. Lindsay also writes newsletters and website content and completed a second novel during lockdown. A history lover, she enjoys cryptic crosswords, dance, long walks in the Peak District and badminton.

Sam Christie is a writer from Aberystwyth. His non-fiction publications include writings on phenomenology, documentary film, the Welsh landscape and a walk he undertook around the far edges of the city of Erbil in Iraqi Kurdistan during the Battle of Mosul in 2016/2017. He began writing long form fiction a year ago and during this time has completed a novella, *The Felling of the Conifers* and the novel *Compass*. He is currently researching his next book which he hopes to finish in the coming year.

Tracy Cook has always loved telling women's stories. At the BBC she directed and produced documentary series, including *Law Women, Medicine Women* and *Children's Hospital*, for which she co-wrote the series' book. While at home in Surrey with her two children, she wrote a blog, *Pass the Sauvignon,* features for *The Times, The Guardian* and several magazines and her unpublished YA novel, *The Slave and the Pharoah's Necklace*. She moved into education PR before taking a novel writing course with Faber. She has now returned to her passion for telling women's stories in her novel, *Room For Doubt*.

Kathryn Ensall has worked as an artist for almost thirty years, exhibiting her paintings internationally. Before that she worked with children in care, and as a secondary school teacher. Her first degree was in English Literature, however, and a few years ago she returned to writing, groping her way through thousands of pages until she found the voice of Jaz, the main character in her first novel, *A Beautiful Girl*. An early manuscript of this novel won the New Voices competition in 2020 and was shortlisted for The Northern Writers Awards. She was born and raised in Rochdale, and now splits her time between North Yorkshire and Sicily.

Gabriel Gane (G.G. Gane) grew up in Wiltshire and the surrounding South-West before graduating from UCA Farnham in Film Production. He's since worked as a freelance video editor, bar tender, shop assistant, awful crepe cook, and unskilled barista. In 2014 he decided to turn his dyslexia into a blunt instrument with which to bludgeon the written word and hasn't looked back. His film articles have been published in *Miniclick* and he has written short stories, flash fiction and haiku. *Thin Skin* is his first novel.

Roger Grant's creative writing evolved from drafting show pitches and scripts for his TV, stage and video productions. He created nationally touring film festivals for MGM and Warner Bros, and later produced *The Greatest Ever Movies* series for Channel Five starring Giles Coren. Inspired one day by an ex-soldier turned operatic street-singer, he wrote and directed the multi-award-winning BBC documentary about his life (www.thepeoplestenor.com). His passion turned to novels, and an unexplained reference to a dark corner of neuroscience by President Obama sparked the idea for his manuscript. GRAY MATTER has been a Finalist for the *William Faulkner-Wisdom Novel Prize*.

Tamara Henriques grew up in Scotland. She studied Japanese at university before moving to New York to work for Condé Nast. This was followed by a short stint at the *Washington Post* and a spell in the UK working in Japanese TV production. Since then, Tamara has lived in Switzerland, Japan, and Hong Kong – where she founded an eponymous fashion label for designer wellington boots. She moved back to the UK in 2016 and started *Portrait of a Family* at the Faber Academy Writing a Novel course in 2017. Tamara lives on a farm in the Cotswolds with her husband and has three children.

Fergal Thomas McHugh has studied literature, philosophy, and computer science, subjects that inspire his writing. He has a Ph.D. in Philosophy and has published on topics at the intersection of philosophy and literature. He lives in Wicklow, Ireland, by the sea. *Polar Terminus* is his first novel.

Mónica Parle was born in the Chihuahuan Desert, which she still considers the home of her heart. For over a century, her family has played hopscotch across the international border between El Paso, Texas, and Ciudad Juarez, Mexico. She grew up among the bayous and roller rinks of southeast Texas, and now lives in London. She is the Co-Executive Director of Forward Arts Foundation and has two novels in progress *The Girl in the Glass House*, which was named the Cornerstone Long-List Award #BNA 2020, and a YA climate-themed adventure novel, which was Highly Commended in Faber's 2018 FAB Prize.

Matthew Putland graduated from Loughborough University in 2019 with a BSc in Sports Science and completed a PGCE at Warwick University in 2020. He taught PE and Science in a secondary school before returning to Loughborough for an MSc in Exercise Medicine. Since starting writing two years ago, Matthew has completed two books in which he uses his love of science to explore real-life problems. His first novel, *Time Will Tell*, grew from his interest in theoretical physics and climate change, and his second novel, *SOLAR*, stems from his love of space exploration and disaster movies. You can find him on Instagram at mjputland.

Gemma Seltzer is a London-based writer. Her work includes the Guardian's award-winning virtual reality film 'Songbird,' fictional blog '5am London' and online flash fiction series 'Speak to Strangers' about conversations with Londoners, subsequently published by Penned in the Margins. She collaborates with dancers, photographers and older adults to create writing and storytelling projects. Gemma has written for BBC Radio 3, performed her work at the Venice Biennale and runs Write & Shine, a programme of early morning writing workshops, events and online courses. Gemma's short fiction collection *Ways of Living* was published by Influx Press in July 2021. Website gemmaseltzer.com

Baljit Sidhu was born and brought up in West Bromwich in the West Midlands. After graduating from Leeds University with a degree in History of Art & English Literature, she spent twenty years producing radio programmes for the BBC. It was while working on longform documentaries on subjects as wide ranging as the influence of Shakespeare on early Indian cinema and the growing rap music scene in Mumbai, she began to consider fiction writing. She began work on her first novel *Bad Luck Face* in 2016. You can find her on Twitter @BalSid2015

Anna Sonny studied French and Spanish and lived in both Córdoba, Spain, and Martinique for a few months as part of her degree. In 2018 she attended writing classes at her local library as part of the Pen to Print creative writing scheme, where she started writing short stories. She began writing her first novel this year on the Write Your Novel course, run by Write Club. She works as a Business Support Manager and is currently also working as a Research Assistant for Paper Nations on a project supporting and creating opportunities for Black writers.

Kim Squirrell grew up in Birmingham and escaped to the countryside at seventeen. She is a west-country artist and writer of Caribbean/Irish heritage with almost as many job titles as birthdays. Publication includes: *Poetry Review*, *Riptide*, *Stand*, and the *Out of Bounds* anthology (Bloodaxe 2012). In 2018 she completed a Creative Writing MA at Exeter, was shortlisted for the Comma Press Dinesh Allirajah prize and commissioned to write for the *Resist* anthology (Comma Press 2019). In crafting a long narrative poem for her dissertation, she acquired the tools to write 'Shale', a story conceived twenty-six years ago on the Exe estuary.

Helga B Viegas was born and raised in Lisbon and moved to London fifteen years ago to find a job and learn tango. Being creative is a compulsion: in the last three years, she has finished two novels and started a short story collection, while enjoying her full-time day job in a digital innovation lab. Helga's list of interests is long and absurd, including shadow puppetry and game theory. She has two MAs in Communications and Design from the University of Lisbon and Central Saint Martins (London) and has completed creative writing courses at City University, London. Website: hbviegas.com

Alexander Whyte is an alumnus of the Faber Academy's 2020 Writing a Novel course. After graduating from the University of Cambridge in 2013 Alex moved to London, where he threw himself into writing as a creative outlet. He is passionate about historical fiction, and how it can explore the origin of themes that still ripple through the world today. Alex finished an unpublished historical novel, *The Alpenstein Affair,* in 2019. He was then selected for the Faber Academy's course to work on his second novel, *The Trinity*. Two years into the project, pirates are now a permanent fixture of his daydreams.

Fiona Williams is a freelance science writer working for the pharmaceutical and health industries. She is also a copyeditor for the journal *Transnational Literature*. She began writing her first novel, *The House of Broken Bricks*, while completing an MA in Creative Writing at Bath Spa University, and the manuscript was shortlisted for the university's Janklow & Nesbit Prize. Born and raised in South-East London, Fiona now lives on a smallholding on the Somerset Levels. She is currently researching her second novel and hopes to embark on a PhD in Creative Writing next year. You can find her on Twitter @FeeWilliams75.